TEMPTED BY THE CEO

IONA ROSE

Get Your FREE Book Here:
https://dl.bookfunnel.com/v9yit8b3f7

Tempted by the CEO

Publisher: Some Books
ISBN- 978-1-913990-23-7

When I see the time, I stand up quickly from my desk. Mr. Connell, CEO of Asima Assets Management, and my direct boss, has a meeting in half an hour that's been flagged as important. I have been told to remind him half an hour before the man is due arrive. I don't want to be even a minute late, because Mr. Connell is the kind of man who notices little things like that.

I walk briskly from my desk to Mr. Connell's office although there isn't much space to cover for me to get there. As Mr. Connell's personal secretary, I am the last line of defence between him and all of the people who want to take up his time. Most people understand that a polite no means just that. But at only five foot three, I'm not exactly intimidating. Yet, I am charged with keeping the people he doesn't want to deal with in the moment away from him.

Working directly for Mr. Connell for two years now, I still find myself nervous every time I have to go into his office. My palms start sweating and I can feel my heart speeding up a little, but over the years, I've learned to hide my nerves well, so no one would ever know I was anything but calm and confident.

I take a half second to study the door while I take a deep breath. The door is a simple light oak bearing the company logo - a circle of red encasing the blue lettering of the company name, the capital letters in a matching red – and a nameplate that reads *Robert Connell, CEO*.

Wiping my palms down my navy blue pencil skirt, I tap on the door. Mr. Connell calls for me to enter. I step inside, a bright smile plastered across my face.

"What is it, Opal?" Mr. Connell asks, looking up from his computer and smiling at me. Mr. Connell is in his early fifties. His black hair is just starting to turn grey around his temples but his grey colored eyes are as sharp as ever. He wears his age well like a good bottle of wine, and he has no shortage of admirers, both in and out of the office.

"You have a meeting in half an hour with Brian Meyers," I say. "You asked for a reminder half an hour before he is due to arrive."

"Thank you." Mr. Connell smiles. "Please call his secretary and confirm."

With a nod, I step back out of his office, pulling his door closed behind me. I mentally add the phone call to my daily to do list and hurry back to my desk. I'd like to call it my office, but truth be told, it's more of a cubby hole. My desk is tucked back into a slight recess a couple of yards down from Mr. Connell's office. It's private enough and the corridor is usually quiet enough for me to work uninterrupted, but I would love an office so I could kick the door shut and keep the world out. It would kind of defeat the purpose of my job though, as a big part of my job is greeting Mr. Connell's associates and potential new clients.

Sitting down at my desk, I turn to my computer. I look up the number for Brian Meyers' secretary, noting that her name is Suzy and I dial her number.

The call is answered on the first ring, "Suzy Hayes, secretary to Mr. Meyers," she says.

Efficient. I like that. "Hi Suzy. This is Opal Collins. I am calling to confirm the eleven o'clock meeting between Mr. Meyers and Mr. Connell of Asima Assets Management."

"Mr. Meyers is currently on his way to the meeting," Suzy assures me.

Thanking her, I end the call. I look at my list of tasks for the day and I know instantly, I'll be working late tonight again. There's no way I can get through all of this before five. I see that tomorrow's schedule is just as busy, so I can't put off any of my tasks. I sigh and pick up the phone to make the first of many calls I have to make.

I have just ended a call when the light on my phone flashes to tell me Mr. Connell is calling me. "Hello," I say, picking up the phone.

"Opal, have you confirmed the meeting like I asked you to?" he says.

"Yes, Mr. Connell," I reply. "I didn't want to disturb you, but the meeting is still going ahead as planned. I would have only felt the need to disturb you if the answer had been a no." Oh God, have I fucked up? Has he been expecting me to let him know either way?

"That's fine. I just wanted to check you'd called already. Mr. Meyers is an extremely difficult man to pin down and to be honest, I was half expecting him to cancel this appointment."

I instantly feel better. I haven't made a mistake. Whew.

Mr. Connell goes on, not waiting for an answer, "Please hold all of my calls until after my meeting. See Mr. Meyers in when he arrives and then make sure I am not disturbed under any circumstances for the duration of the meeting," he says.

"Yes, Mr. Connell." I resist the urge to tell him I would never allow him to be disturbed during a meeting. I don't really know a lot about Mr. Meyers or his company or why he's having a meeting with Mr. Connell. But it must be important if Mr. Connell feels the need to point out something so obvious to me. I have to admit I'm curious about the whole thing. As Mr. Connell's personal secretary, I usually get to know what his meetings are about, but this one is like some top-secret mission where I haven't been told anything really, except Mr. Meyers' name and his company name.

I shake my head slightly. I don't have time to be distracted by trying to work out exactly what's going on here. It's none of my business and if at some point down the line, I do need to know about it, then I know I will be told.

Tending to another two calls, I fend off three calls for Mr. Connell, taking down the details and promising to pass them on once Mr. Connell is out of his meeting. While typing up some letters, I hear footsteps coming along the corridor. I look up from my typing to see a man I don't recognize, making his way along the corridor towards me.

A little on the short side, he looks to be about the same age as Mr. Connell, although the years haven't been quite as kind to him. He has a little bit of a paunch and his hair line is receding. He's wearing a very expensive looking suit.

I wonder briefly if it's to compensate for his hair line. I tell myself to stop being a bitch as I stand up and extend my hand. "Mr. Meyers, I presume?" I smile.

He shakes my outstretched hand. He has a firm grip, but his palm is slightly sweaty. His sweaty palm makes him seem nervous, as does the slight twitch in his right eye. He smiles at me as he nods his head curtly, but the smile doesn't reach his eyes.

"I'm Opal Collins," I greet him. "Mr. Connell's secretary. If you'd like to follow me please." I step around in front of Mr. Meyers and lead him towards Mr. Connell's office. My own palms remain dry, my confidence buoyed by the nerves of Mr. Meyers.

Knocking on Mr. Connell's office door, I push it open when he shouts for me to come in. I stand back and gesture for Mr. Meyers to enter. "Your eleven o'clock Mr. Connell," I smile. "Would you like any refreshments brought in?"

"No thank you," Mr. Connell replies, answering for both men as he stands up to shake Mr. Meyers' hand. "That will be all, Opal."

With a nod, I step out of the office and gently close the door. I'm tempted to remain in place and see if I can work out who the mysterious Mr. Meyers is and why he clearly doesn't want to be here, but I decide against it. It would be the height of unprofessional and I would be fired instantly if caught.

I return to my desk and try to forget about my curiosity. It doesn't take long for me to lose myself in finishing typing up the letters.

When I hear footsteps approaching, I steel myself for an argument when I tell whoever it is that Mr. Connell is unavailable but I relax when I see it's just Jessie, one of the other secretaries.

She's practically skipping along the corridor, her auburn curls bouncing on her shoulders as she approaches. She's grinning, a wide grin that makes her eyes sparkle.

I know that look. It's the look that says she has something particularly juicy to share with me. I feel a mild streak of annoyance run through me at the interruption for something that clearly isn't going to be about the business, but I decide to hear Jessie out.

Reaching my desk, she plonks herself down in the chair opposite mine. She's so excitable she reminds me of a puppy. All she needs to do is start panting. "Guess what," she says, her eyes shining with excitement. She can't keep still on the chair, her whole body shifting constantly. She reaches up with one hand and twirls a curl around her finger.

"What?" I ask, smiling despite my earlier annoyance as I feel myself getting pulled in to her excitement.

"You have to guess," she insists.

I roll my eyes. "You got a promotion?"

She shakes her head.

"You were right about Martha from accounts sleeping with the mail man?"

"Yes, I was right about that, but that's not it," Jessie gushes.

"God Jess, I don't know. Have you won the lottery or something?"

Jessie laughs, a musical sound that is infectious.

Now, I feel the last bit of annoyance leave me, even though part of me wants to shake her to get her to cut to the chase.

"Honestly Opal, you are so bad at this game," she says shaking her head.

Even my lack of game playing skills don't keep her down for long though and she grins again as she finally reveals her news, "Word is that the ever elusive Brett Connell, Mr. Connell's son, has just pulled into the parking garage."

"Rightttt," I say, drawing the word out into a question. How the hell would I have guessed that? And why is Jessie so excited about it? I mean I know Brett is rather elusive to say the least, but still. After two years of working directly for Mr. Connell, I have never met nor spoken to his son. But then is that so weird? Brett's a grown man. He probably has his own life that doesn't involve coming to see his father at work.

I've heard plenty of rumours about Brett. Everything from him being the black sheep of the family who did time in juvie as a teenager to him being a recluse who refuses to leave his home. The truth is probably neither of those things. Obviously, the latter isn't true, or he wouldn't be here now. And if the former was true, Jessie would already have spilled all of the details of it to me.

None of this really helps to explain why Jessie is so excited about this though. Or why she thinks I will care about the news. "Seriously Opal, try to at least pretend to be excited." She laughs.

"Ok," I say. "I'm excited. There... I pretended. Now why is this something you're so excited about?"

"Now, I am offended." Jessie tries to give me a pout, but is unable to stop herself from smiling. "I'm just shocked you even have to ask. But then in your defense, you haven't seen Brett before, have you?"

I shake my head.

Jessie fans herself with her hand, as she gets up from the chair and starts to walk away. She turns back to grin at me. "I'm going to go and pretend I need to take the elevator some-where, so I can be there when he gets out. Once you see him, you'll understand my excitement. Brace yourself Opal. You are about to see the most beautiful man who ever existed."

Laughing softly and shaking my head, I can't help but wonder what this guy is going to look like to have her that excited about his arrival. I mean is he made of gold or something?

I guess I'm about to find out. Jessie has only been gone from my desk for a couple of minutes when I hear the ping of the elevator arriving and I know it'll be mere seconds before the door opens. It doesn't necessarily mean it's this Brett guy, but a couple of seconds later, I hear Jessie laughing in a flirty way. I smile to myself as I picture her tossing her hair back and laughing hysterically at something that is, at best, mildly amusing probably.

Pretending to be fixated on my computer screen, although I have completely lost track of the figures, I wait just a few seconds. I then realize I'll have to start over again. *Great.*

Thanks for that Jessie. I can't put all of the blame on Jessie though. I should have had more sense than to let myself get pulled into the conversation, but Jessie is a good friend and I have to admit I enjoy her cheerful personality. It keeps office life interesting.

I glance up without moving my head when I hear quick, quiet footsteps approaching. I don't see much. I don't let my eyes linger in case he catches me looking at him. All I see is a flash of a grey suit and that the man is tall. I mean everyone is tall compared to me, but he must be over six feet tall. He has a definite presence, a confidence that I can almost feel as he moves towards me, and despite myself, my breath catches a little in my throat.

Keeping my eyes glued on my screen again, until Brett is almost at my desk, I know it would be rude not to acknowledge him at this point. His cologne fills my nostrils, a woodsy, spicy scent that should be overpowering but somehow isn't. As I turn my eyes up to look at him, I try to forget Jessie's words and her excitement.

I smile up at him, flashing him my polished, customer service smile. It freezes on my face when I finally allow myself to look at Brett properly. Jessie wasn't exaggerating about Brett's looks. In fact, calling him the most beautiful man I would ever see actually feels like she's sold him short a little bit.

The man is that fucking hot.

He looks like he's around thirty-five, certainly no older than that. With thick dark hair in a trendy style that manages to look tousled and casual like he hasn't made any effort with it at all, and yet perfectly styled and in place at the same time. Staring at his full, thick hair, I imagine myself pushing my fingers into it as his lips move to meet mine. It would be silky soft, the kind of hair you want to touch constantly and can never get enough of.

I force myself to look away from his hair, feeling my cheeks turning pink as I shake off the image of my hands in his hair, his lips on mine. It turns out that looking away from his hair is a mistake. It had been distracting, but it has nothing compared to his eyes. They're the color of caramel, a warm brown that makes me melt inside. His eyes are so mesmerising that I can't look away from them, and the longer I look at them, the more detail I see. They're flecked with tiny specks of lighter brown, a color that is almost gold the flecks catch the light and sparkle as though they really are tiny pieces of gold leaf floating there in his eyes.

The gold flecks make me think of my earlier thought when I wondered if the man was made of gold or something. It turns out I wasn't wrong, except that next to him, gold would look like cheap copper. Something to be tossed aside in favor of the much better thing beside it.

Brett clears his throat.

Now, I feel the slight flush on my face when I realize just how long I've been staring at him. Wow, Jessie was so right about him. I should have been more prepared, so I could play it cool.

Instead, I stare at Brett and I realize with horror that I'm still staring at him. Even as my mind screams at me to look away from him, I just can't quite bring myself to do it. And to make matters worse, my mouth is still frozen in my fake, customer service smile. My cheeks are actually starting to ache from the smile. I must look like I have a damned coat hanger wedged in my mouth.

Could this get any worse? I mean I guess I could have set him on fire or something, but on a normal scale of things, where arson isn't a player, then no, it really couldn't be going much worse at all.

I finally manage to force my eyes away from him. Well, not away from him exactly, but I manage to stop staring into his eyes like some extra from a bad soap opera, and at least move my gaze down to this mouth. It's no safer really, all I can think of when I look at his lips is how they will taste sweet. Now, I don't think I'll ever be able to speak again.

Brett smiles at me and there's nothing fake about his smile. It makes his eyes light up and it takes everything I have not to stare into them again. His teeth are straight and white, like something from a tooth paste commercial and I can't help but wonder absently if he's ever done any modelling.

"Hi. I'm Brett Connell," he says as he holds his hand out to me.

Suddenly, I realize with horror that he wants to shake my hand. But my palm is disgustingly sweaty by now and I can't exactly wipe it down on my skirt without him noticing. I shyly extend my hand and he envelopes it in his large, dry hand. I wait for him to pull away in disgust, but to his credit, he shakes my hand like it's normal to touch a stranger's sopping wet palm and his expression doesn't change. He must know the effect he has on women. There's no way he can look like this and not know about it. He probably had been expecting my palm to be wet. I don't know if this makes it better or worse, but I don't waste any energy worrying about it.

As my hand is enveloped in his, I feel a bolt of lightning burst through my body, lighting me up from the inside out. It's as though his touch wakes something up inside of me. The lightning bolt spreads through my body, heading straight for my clit which tingles and makes me press my thighs together.

Brett releases my hand.

I hear myself make a quiet *ahh* sound. I hope he hasn't heard it. If he has, he doesn't comment on it, but he's not going to is he? He probably thinks I'm his father's charity project, like he's doing some sort of outreach where he employs mental cases or something. I mean I am sweaty, mesmerised by him, and still completely mute. What else is he supposed to think? Even if he knows he has an effect on women, he can't think this is normal.

"I'm here to see Robert Connell," Brett adds.

I find it odd that he refers to his father so formally and somehow, that breaks the spell and I find my voice again. "Mr. Connell is in a very important meeting right now." My voice comes out low and breathy. It's not like my normal voice, but I kind of like it. It's kind of sexy and at least it's not shaky or weird. "He doesn't want to be disturbed, but you're more than welcome to wait. I can show you to an empty office if you would like?"

Brett frowns ever so slightly and shakes his head.

During our whole exchange, his eyes have been on me, on my face, on my chest. I should be either offended or flattered, I can't decide which, but instead, I'm mortified. Of course, he's watching me. He's probably waiting for the crazy girl to jump up and try and kiss him or something and he wants to be prepared so he can duck away in time to avoid me.

"No thank you," Brett says.

I don't know whether I'm relieved he's going to leave, so I can stop embarrassing myself, or whether I'm gutted he's going to leave because I'll most likely, never get another chance to see him again.

"I'll see him now," he adds. He half turns and starts towards his father's office door.

I jump to my feet. "You can't go in there!"

Brett glances back over his shoulder and gives me a lopsided smile. "Is that so?" he grins.

His grin makes my pussy clench and my heart race. I nod, momentarily mute again. "Yes... I," I start, but I'm too late.

Brett's hand is already on the door handle of Mr. Connell's office and before I can utter another word, he pushes the door open and goes inside.

Oh God, I am in so much trouble here.

Stepping back behind my desk, I sit down heavily. I have barely sat down when Brian Meyers storms out of the office. I open my mouth to say something to try and make this better, but he doesn't even glance in my direction as he marches past me. I can see his face is full of thunder and I don't know what to do to fix it. There's really no fixing this.

I might as well just start packing my things because I can't see Mr. Connell accepting the fact that I let someone disturb him and pissed off Mr. Meyers like that. I put my face in my hands for a moment, resting my elbows on my desk. I swallow hard, trying to work out what I'm going to say to Mr. Connell when he demands an explanation for this. I can hardly say I was so distracted by Brett's looks that I was too late to stop him when I realized his intentions.

Goddammit. I've screwed up so big here and for what? A smile from a handsome stranger. Was it worth it? The worst part is that a big part me thinks it was.

I slowly peel my hands away from my face when I realize I can hear yelling coming from Mr. Connell's office. I know I shouldn't eavesdrop, but it's hardly eavesdropping when two people are shouting loud enough for me to hear them through a closed door and all the way to my desk. I condone staying right where I am by telling myself I'm in enough trouble for letting Brett slip by me, without also being missing from my desk if Mr. Connell comes looking for me.

"You realize you've just cost this firm what could have been a very lucrative deal?" Mr. Connell shouts.

"Don't worry father," Brett retaliates. He says the word *father* like it's an insult. "I'm sure your ass kissing skills will come into play and save the deal. You seem to be very good at getting people to do what you want them to do."

"Except seemingly my own receptionist because if she did as I said, you wouldn't be in here," Mr. Connell shoots back.

Fuck. I'm about to get the head's up that I'm going to be fired.

"Oh, bullshit, Brett shouts back. "Don't even try to blame this on her. You knew I'd come down here when I heard what you'd done and you knew it would take more than her to stop me!"

Butterflies now whirl around in my stomach. Brett is defending me. I bite my lip to keep from smiling. I catch myself. It's hardly a time for me to be sitting here smiling.

Brett goes on, "Don't pretend like you didn't want this to happen. If you didn't, then you would have had security out there, not a damned receptionist."

"I made the mistake of thinking you would act like a professional and not come barging into a meeting," Mr. Connell exclaims. "I should have known better. But yeah, you're right, that was my mistake, not Opal's."

Ok, maybe I'm not getting fired after all. Assuming I can actually focus enough to get some work done. I can't though. Not yet. I accept that I will be working even later tonight than I first thought. I have to hear how this all pans out. And then, I'll have to pretend like I didn't hear a thing when I go to Mr. Connell's office and apologize for letting Brett get past me. I'm already starting to plan out what I will say to get around all of this, but I'm mostly focused on the argument that's still raging in Mr. Connell's office.

"Act like a professional? That's rich coming from you," Brett shouts.

"What the hell is that supposed to mean?" Mr. Connell yells.

"I think you know, but if you want, I'll spell it out to you," Brett says. "You sabotaged my deal, thinking it would leave me with no choice but to come and work for you. But let me tell you something. I would rather flip burgers in a fucking McDonald's than come here to work for you."

"Oh son," Mr. Connell replies. His voice is taunting, like he's trying to goad Brett into getting angrier. "It's cute that you would think that, but let me spell this out for you, because I think it's you that's missing something here. I didn't sabotage your deal. Your deal was shit, so the company saw that and pulled out of their own accord. And as for you working here? There's no chance of that. I'm afraid I only take the best and that deal and your reaction to losing it, tells me that's not you. I can't work with people who have this whole victim mentality going on. Admit it. You screwed up and now, you're just looking for someone to blame."

I hear a loud crashing sound and I think one of them must have thrown that ugly Ming vase that Mr. Connell loves so much.

"Really? You're not even going to have the balls to admit to what you did? Honestly, I expected better," Brett barks. "If you weren't involved, then why would you have been expecting me? And don't say you weren't. You admitted it when you said you thought I would have waited until after your meeting to come in here."

"I wasn't involved. But I knew you'd come here, because you always come to me when you need someone to blame your mistakes on to," Mr. Connell retorts.

"For fuck's sake," Brett shouts back. "You're really going to stand there and deny this with that smug grin on your face? I should have known you'd do this. You've never taken responsibility for anything in your life."

"Oh, so now you're making this about your mother? You sound just like her," Mr. Connell snaps.

"Well, it could be worse. I could sound like you," Brett shouts.

The door to Mr. Connell's office slams open.

I quickly begin typing. I am typing nonsense on a blank document, anything to look like I wasn't sitting here eavesdropping.

But I needn't have worried. Brett marches past me without so much as a glance in my direction and Mr. Connell slams his office door closed, and the fact there are no footsteps tells me he's stayed on the inside of the door.

It looks like I've dodged the bullet, but I know I need to knuckle down and get through my work. I also know I need to pretend like I didn't hear any of that when Mr. Connell is ready to talk to me. But I am more than a little intrigued as to what just happened.

It's clear to me that Mr. Connell and his son don't get along, but I can't help but to wonder why. And why Mr. Connell was so adamant that he didn't want Brett to work here. He's never made any secret of that fact he always wanted his son to take over the firm, but Brett declined the offer. Has he really changed his mind, or there is something else going on here?

I have so many questions about the ever mesmerizing, mysterious Brett, but I probably will know any of the answers.

1

Opal

One Year Later

"Yes, I know," I say into the phone pressed between my ear and my shoulder. "I realize it's inconvenient Mr. Hall, but unfortunately there's very little I can do at this point, except apologize again."

I'm bent over at the car door as I gather up a pile of files with my ass in the air, dragging them towards me from the passenger seat. I really am regretting taking this call. I should have known better. If my voice mail explaining that Mr. Connell is in hospital, following a heart attack did not placate this man, then nothing would.

Instead, Mr. Hall just seems to want to berate me for a while for something that isn't my fault. "Your apology isn't going to get my meeting happening any faster though is it, Miss?" he says.

And neither is your damned attitude. That's what I want to say, but of course, I don't. Instead, I bite my tongue and agree with Mr. Hall in what I hope is a sympathetic tone, "No Mr. Hall, but as I explained in my voice mail, there really isn't anything more I can tell you at this point. As soon as I have any further information about the situation, I promise that you will be the first to know."

That's a lie. He will be told eventually, but after all of the clients who haven't bitten my head off over this.

I finally manage to get all of the files and papers gathered together and into my arms. I juggle them rather precariously while I fumble my car keys back out of my jacket pocket. I kick the door closed and press the button to lock my car, and then I turn and hurry across the parking area. Mr. Hall's voice is still banging on in my ear and I'm trying my best to think of something to say to make him shut up and go away, Since my voicemail to him didn't do that, then I'm really at a loss for what will.

Hearing a loud beeping of a car horn followed by the screech of tyres, I look to my right where the noise came from. I'm expecting to see two drivers squaring up to each other, each one blaming the other for pulling out on them. Instead, I am horrified to see a car speeding towards me. I freeze, biting back a scream as the files go flying from my hands.

Dammit. Dammit. And double fucking dammit.

The car manages to stop inches in front of me and I let out a shaky breath. I can feel tears starting to well up in my eyes and my hand is shaking as I reach up for the phone. "Mr. Hall," I say, cutting him off midsentence. "I'm sorry, I really can't talk right now. I'll call you as soon as I have any further information for you."

I cut off the call even though he's still talking. I know I will get a load of flak for that if Mr. Connell finds out, but right now, I really don't care. I almost got killed because of being distracted by Mr. Hall and his incessant complaints. Right now, all I want to do is go back to my car, go home, and curl up under the blankets. I can't do that of course, but I can at least stop the man's whining in my ear.

My phone rings almost immediately after I end the call. Mr. Hall's name flashes on the screen, and before I can change my mind, I turn the phone off and drop it into my pocket. I crouch down and begin to retrieve the files. Papers have flown from them and they're everywhere, all of the carefully organized documents are scattered around in a total disorganized mess.

The driver of the car who almost hit me lays on his horn.

I can feel my temper rising. The bastard nearly hit me with his car, and now he can't wait two fucking minutes while I retrieve my things?

I keep grabbing the papers, shutting out the blaring horn. I hear the window slide down and I glance up to see a man's head poking out of the driver's side window.

His face is red and he's frowning. "Do you think you could take a little longer there?" he snaps.

"I'm fine, thanks for asking," I snap back, glaring at him. I go back to retrieving my papers. My anger, the fact I could have been killed, and the pressure from the driver all add together to make me clumsy and slower than I normally would have been.

"Jeez lady, some of us have places to be you know," the driver shouts.

"For the love of God, can you give me a fucking minute?" I shout. "Either come and help me, or close the window and shut the fuck up."

I'm a little surprised when I hear the window go back up. I half expected him to jump out of his car and forcibly move me out of the way. I finish gathering the papers together, the process being a little quicker now, since the driver isn't hurling abuse at me. I finally straighten up and I dash the rest of the way across the parking lot. I don't glance back at the car, not even when the driver opens his window again, and calls me a bitch as he speeds away.

Finally, I manage to enter the hospital just about in one piece. I take a moment to look around the sterile looking lobby area, taking in the familiar scent of a hospital. It smells like a combination of antiseptic and stewing vegetables. I guess even having the money to check into one of the best private hospitals in the city can't hide the fact it is indeed still a hospital.

Wrinkling my nose at the smell, I head towards the reception desk that's tucked into an alcove inside of the entranceway. "Hi," I say, smiling at the woman. "I'm looking for Robert Connell."

After the morning I've had, I half expect her to say good luck with that or something equally sarcastic, but instead, she types the name into her computer and smiles up at me. "He's in room 356. Take the elevator to the third floor and go to your right. The elevators are just at the end of this corridor."

"Thank you," I say.

I debate sitting down on one of the benches that line the corridor and rearranging all of my papers back into their proper order first, but I'm already late and I decide against it. I hurry into the first elevator that stops and ride up to the third floor. I turn right as instructed. I make my way along the corridor, peering into windows as I pass them, looking for Mr. Connell.

A nurse approaches from the opposite direction. She smiles questioningly at me.

"I'm looking for Robert Connell," I tell her when it becomes clear to me that she isn't going to move on without some sort of explanation as to what I'm doing here.

She leads me to a busy nurse's station and looks at a printed sheet that's on the desk. "Are you family?" she asks.

"No," I say. "I work with Mr. Connell. He asked me to drop some things off for him." I gesture down to the messy pile of papers in my arms and I'm sure I see the nurse wince at the state of them.

"What's your name?" she asks me.

"Opal Collins," I say.

She looks back down at her list and nods her head. "I can see your name on the approved visitors list. Bear with me one moment please." She moves away and taps on a door and goes into the room. She leaves it ajar.

I hear the conversation they have.

"Mr. Connell? Opal Collins is here to see you," the nurse says.

"About damned time," Mr. Connell interrupts her. He's noticed I'm late then and he sounds kind of angry.

I cringe.

"I assume the papers she's carrying are some sort of work related thing. I must reiterate that you are meant to be resting, Mr. Connell," the nurse says in a patient voice she is probably using to mask her frustration with Mr. Connell's blatant disregard for her instructions.

"Noted," Mr. Connell says. "Please send Opal in."

"Robert ..." a female voice that I assume belongs to Mrs. Connell says in a warning tone.

"Don't Robert me. It's more stressful for me to not know what's going on with the company than it is for me to see Opal for ten minutes. Nurse, please send her in," Mr. Connell says again.

I wait for the nurse or Mrs. Connell to argue with him, but it seems they've seen what I've known for years. It's easier to do things his way than it is to argue with him.

The nurse steps back out of the room and nods to me. "You can go in. Please don't do anything to stress the patient, and don't be in there too long okay?"

I nod, although I'm pretty sure one look at the mess of papers in my arms is going to have Mr. Connell's blood pressure off the charts. I move towards the door and tap on it although it's still ajar.

"Come in, come in," Mr. Connell says, gesturing through the crack in the door for me to hurry up.

I step inside the room.

Mr. Connell is sitting up in bed wearing a light blue pyjama jacket. He looks a lot better than I expected him to – he's not pasty looking or anything – and to be honest, if I didn't know he was ill, I would never have believed it.

He smiles warmly at me as I approach the bed.

"I'm so sorry I'm late," I say. "The traffic was manic and then I nearly got hit by a car in the car park and I dropped all of the files." I trail off, holding the files up for Mr. Connell to see.

He frowns and shakes his head. "It's fine Opal. I knew you would have a good reason for being late, and it's only a few minutes. I'm just tetchy because I'm stuck in here. I wasn't really annoyed with you. Did you say you almost got hit by a car?" He pauses.

I nod sheepishly.

"Are you okay? Do you want me to ask one of the nurses to look you over?" he says.

"No, honestly I'm fine. I was just a bit shocked," I say.

His whole demeanor has changed since he beckoned me impatiently into his room. I really should have used the, *I almost got killed on my way here* line before. "Just give me a minute to sort through all of this and get it into some sort of order," I say.

Mr. Connell shakes his head again. "Don't worry about it Opal. Honestly, sorting through it all will give me something to do while I'm stuck in here."

Mrs. Connell is sitting beside the bed dressed in black slacks and a cream colored floral print blouse. Her hair is pinned up in a neat French pleat. She's wearing a pretty gold chain with matching bracelet and earrings.

Her husband just had a heart attack and she looks more put together than I feel right now. But hey, she didn't almost get killed getting here presumably.

"You already have something do while you're here," Mrs. Connell says firmly. "You heard the doctor. You're here to rest, not sort out your secretary's mishaps." Mrs. Connell is completely focused on her husband right now and him on her.

He glares at her.

I really don't want to be the cause of an argument between the two of them. "Really it's fine. I'll sort the papers." I start towards the bed, needing somewhere to spread the files out so I can rearrange the loose papers.

Mr. Connell glances at me and shakes his head as he turns back to his wife. "Yes, the doctor says I should rest. But it's not his business that will go to shit while I'm laid here reading or watching the TV is it?"

Mrs. Connell opens her mouth to reply, most likely to remind him none of this will matter if he works himself into an early grave.

"Listen Yvonne," Mr. Connell cuts her off before she can get started. "I appreciate your concern, I really do. But right now, I have to focus. Why don't you be a dear and go down to the cafeteria and fetch us all a decent cup of coffee or something?" He says it gently, but it's clear that it's not really a request.

Mrs. Connell is being dismissed and she knows it. She holds Mr. Connell's gaze for a moment.

I squirm awkwardly as I wait for her to argue with him. I'm debating whether I should just dump the files on Mr. Connell's bed and slip away.

Mrs. Connell finally responds. "Fine," she snaps, finally looking away from Mr. Connell. She gets up and storms towards the door to Mr. Connell's room, making sure to give me a severe look.

I can read that look easily. *When he called and asked for the files, you should have said no. If he dies, it's your fault.*

"See if you can talk some sense into him, because I as sure as hell can't," she says as she steps out into the corridor.

"Relax, it'll be a fine," a voice replies.

It's a male voice, one vaguely familiar to me, but I don't think I know anyone who works at this hospital. I didn't notice anyone in the room besides my boss and his wife, so I am a bit startled.

"Right, hand me those files please Opal," Mr. Connell says.

As I step towards the bed, a shadow falls over me while I hand them over then turn, waiting for a lecture from a doctor or a nurse for bringing Mr. Connell's work here. Instead, I find myself face to face with Brett, Mr. Connell's prodigal son who I haven't seen for a year since he came into the office and argued with his father and then left the building without so much as glancing at me.

He's doing a little more than glancing at me now. His eyes sweep over my face and then lock onto mine as he smiles at me.

2

I t's suddenly like no time has passed at all since I last saw Brett, as he has the same mesmerising effect on me. I try to look away from him, but I can't. It's like his gaze is paralyzing me, but in the nicest possible way. I can barely breathe and I can feel my clit throbbing as I stare into those beautiful golden brown eyes.

He doesn't look a day older than the last time I last saw him and his hair has the same effortless look, in a tousled style as it did that day. I instinctively curl my hands into fists at my sides, stopping myself from even being tempted to reach out and touch his thick, luscious looking hair.

"Don't even think about lecturing me about working," Mr. Connell says from behind me.

The spell is broken and I look away. I find I can breathe again as take in a breath that is a little louder than I would have liked it to be. I can feel my insides turning to jelly and my cheeks flushing.

Mr. Connell looks at me as Brett assures him he's not here to try to convince him of anything, because he knows he would be wasting his time.

"Good," Mr. Connell says. "Do you remember Opal? She was my secretary when you last came by the building."

"I remember her." He looks at me and smiles again.

This time, I'm slightly more prepared to face him and I return the smile with a tentative smile of my own.

"Opal is one of my most valued employees. Treat her that way. She's my personal assistant now, and she knows the company almost as well as I do. If you need anything, you go to Opal, because if she doesn't know the answer to any questions you might have, then I guarantee you that no one at the company does," Mr. Connell says to Brett. He turns his attention to me. "Opal, this is my son, Brett Connell. He'll be taking over running the company for a short time until I'm back on my feet."

I extend my hand to Brett, knowing it's the appropriate response to the formal introduction, especially since I've been told he's going to be my boss. I'm already anticipating the sparks that will fly when Brett takes my hand in his and I just hope I can hide my reaction from both men.

Brett smiles again and shakes my hand.

His grip is warm and firm, just like I remembered it to be, and at least this time, my palm is reasonably dry. The spark of lightning flies through my body, just like I knew it would and I feel a longing in my lower belly that I have a feeling only Brett can fulfil.

He nods to his father, releasing my hand.

I wish that would break the spell he has me under, but it doesn't. My palm still tingles where he touched it. My fingers still feel as though I can feel his against them.

"Got it." Brett picks up the top file from the pile beside his father on the bed and sits down in the chair his mother was sitting in. He opens the file and begins to flick through it.

I manage to drag my eyes away from him for a moment, but they instantly go back to him. He's so damned hot. His mouth is slightly pursed as he concentrates on the information in the file and I suddenly wish Mr. Connell wasn't here. Then I would be able to really study Brett and drink him in while he's distracted.

"Ok Opal. Where are we with the Graham deal?" Mr. Connell asks.

His voice pulls my attention away from Brett, as I perch on the end of Mr. Connell's bed and begin to tell him the latest on the Graham deal.

He nods as I talk, taking occasional notes.

I'm very much aware of the exact moment Brett stops looking at the file and starts taking notice of what I am telling Mr. Connell. I feel my cheeks growing red again, and I start to fumble my words.

If Mr. Connell notices, he's too polite to ask me about it.

The whole time we're talking, I can feel Brett's eyes on me. He doesn't interrupt and the odd time Mr. Connell directs a comment in his direction when there's something he particularly needs to know, he speaks with a stilted formality, as though he's talking to a stranger.

It makes me curious and I'm dying to ask them about it, but I know for a fact that's not a good idea and naturally, I hold off from asking about it. "I think that's everything pressing," I say finally.

I've been talking long enough for Mrs. Connell to come back with coffee for everyone, even me. She is still short with me, making it clear that she thinks this whole impromptu business meeting is my fault. I wish I could tell her the truth; that right now, I'd give anything to be back at work, safely tucked away in my office, away from Brett's scrutinizing gaze that makes my insides tilt.

She sits in the corner of the room, a sulky look on her face.

"Did you catch all of that Brett?" Mr. Connell asks.

"Yes," Brett replies.

"Have you got any questions about any of it?" Mr. Connell presses him.

Brett shakes his head. "Nope. And I know – if I run into any problems, I'll ask Opal."

I love the way my name sounds on his lips. I've never really liked my name. I was named after my mother's grandmother. The name is so old fashioned and I've always cringed when I introduce myself to anyone, but on Brett's lips, it sounds modern and exotic. Exhilarating even. "Is that everything then Mr. Connell?" I ask.

"Almost," he says with a smile. "I love that you're so keen to get back to work. Mind you, if Yvonne was glaring at me the way she keeps glaring at you, I'd be in a rush to get away too."

I gasp slightly as he draws attention to the fact that Yvonne is still giving me the death glare.

She turns the glare to him, but then she blushes slightly and when she looks back away from Mr. Connell, she looks down into her lap rather than back at me.

I clear my throat, trying to break the uncomfortable silence that's fallen over the room.

"There's just the dinner party to arrange," Mr. Connell says.

I panic for a second. He expects me to throw a dinner party? I'm pretty sure that's way above my pay grade.

He must see my expression because he gives a soft laugh. "Relax Opal. It's a party, not a death sentence. It's tomorrow night. William Harley is throwing it. Remember?"

I nod, instantly knowing what he's talking about. He doesn't expect me to throw a dinner party. He's referring to the one being thrown by William Hardy, a long term client. Mr. Connell has been invited to the dinner party. "I remember," I say. "I'll call him and let him know you won't be able to make it as soon as I get back to the office."

"Tell him Brett will be attending in my place," Mr. Connell says.

Brett raises an eyebrow in his direction.

"It's not optional Brett. There will be some big players there and it's a good way to get some new contracts. Opal, you will be attending as Brett's plus one to make sure he speaks to the right people about the right things," Mr. Connell says.

"I'm quite capable of working out for myself who I want to speak to," Brett states quietly.

"I'm sure you are," Mr. Connell agrees. "But I have a few leads I've been warming up over the last few months and Opal knows who is who and what's been said. It's not just idle mingling Brett."

"Whatever," Brett says.

"Opal?" Mr. Connell says.

I nod mutely, suddenly afraid my voice won't come out, even if I try to speak. I don't know whether I'm excited or nervous to learn that I'll be spending an evening with the mysterious Brett at an actual party.

It's just work, I remind myself, but it's like my body doesn't quite get the memo my brain is sending it, because it's all I can do not to punch the air in excitement.

3

I am so nervous that my hand is shaking when I bring it up to my face to apply my lip gloss. I grab my wrist with my other hand to steady it and brush the gloss onto my lips. I smile in approval when I manage to get it on without smearing it around my face or getting it on my teeth.

Glancing at the clock as I cross the apartment, I see I have about half an hour before I'm due to be picked up. My makeup is on and my hair is done. I'm wearing my hair half up and half down, the top half twisted and pinned in place, with small tendrils hanging around my face. I slip into my room and move to my wardrobe where I stand staring at the clothes there, trying to decide what to wear.

The event is black tie and I want to look the part. I want Brett to see me outside of work, in something other than pencil skirts and trouser suits. I want him to see me and think *wow*. I also want to look the part so I don't let Mr. Connell down. He has a very strict policy of impressing clients, which includes dressing appropriately for any event.

I think for a moment and then I pull out a short green dress. I slip it on, enjoying the satiny feel of it against my skin. I frown into the mirror, unsure about the dress now. It looks good. It shows off my tanned legs, but it's a little lower cut than I remember it and I'm not sure that showing my legs and so much cleavage is a good idea at a business event.

The door to the apartment opens and I relax. My roommate Rita is home from work and she's always had way more fashion sense than me. She'll know if this is appropriate or not. I move to the door and pull it open, standing in the doorway without a word.

Rita looks up as the door opens. She grins when she sees me and whistles. "Well, look at you all dressed up. You look gorgeous Opal," she smiles.

"Thanks." I smile, feeling better about the dress.

"Big date?" she asks.

I shake my head. I wish it was a date. Any kind of date with Brett would work for me. "No. It's that dinner party I told you about."

"The one for work with your boss's son?" she asks with a raised eyebrow.

I nod again.

She shakes her head, grinning. "So you're trying to seduce Brett?"

"What? No!" I shriek.

She raises her eyebrow higher.

I laugh. Rita knows me far too well for me to pretend like I haven't been dreaming of seducing Brett ever since I first set eyes on him a year ago. "Ok, I'd very much like to. But not tonight. Tonight is strictly business. There's a few potential clients Mr. Connell wants me to introduce Brett to."

"Well, unless you're trying to seduce all of them, then I suggest you change," she says.

"Really?" I ask, a little disappointed.

"Really," she confirms. "Opal, if you honestly thought the dress was right for the occasion, you wouldn't have presented yourself to me like that and waited for my critique."

"Ugh, you're so damned observant," I say with a half smile.

She laughs and shoos me back into the bedroom. "Less is more Opal. And I don't mean less material. I mean find something that looks professional and appropriate, but gives Brett just a little hint as to what's underneath it."

I nod and go back into the bedroom. I slip out of the green dress and hang it back up. I stare into my wardrobe again. I don't think I have anything even remotely close to what Rita is describing. I'm getting frustrated. I'm going to end up having to go in a sensible work outfit and although it will be appropriate, it will hardly put me in a good light with Brett.

Just as I am about to give up, I spot a black dress at the back of my closet. One I had completely forgotten about. I fell in love with it and bought it on sale, telling myself I would find an event to wear it to, but I never ever did. It would be perfect for tonight though. I reach in and rub it between my fingers as I nod to myself and pull it out and put it on. I look into the full length mirror in the corner and I know it's the right dress without even having to ask Rita.

It's a long dress with splits either side that run to my mid thigh. It's enough to do what Rita said; look appropriate, but give just a hint of what lies beneath. The dress clings to my body, showing off my curvy hips and flat stomach. The straps are spaghetti straps and the neck line is high enough to be proper, but low enough to again, give just a hint of what lies beneath it. It will definitely show Brett a side to me he's never seen before.

A side I hope he likes. I smile to myself and shake my head as I look for the right shoes to wear. I'm acting like this is a date and it really isn't. As if someone like Brett would even notice someone like me, let alone want to date me. I tell myself the dress isn't really for him, it's for me. I want to look good and yes, I want him to notice me, but deep down, I know nothing will ever happen between us.

Even if he is into me, it would be wholly inappropriate since he's my boss, and if Mr. Connell ever found out, I'd be fired for sure.

I find my trusty black heels and slip them on. I add a pair of silver dangly earrings and a silver necklace that hangs to just where my cleavage starts. I grab my matching purse and push my stuff into it and then I go back out into the living room again.

Rita is lying on her belly on the couch reading a magazine, her hair hanging in her face. She reaches up and pushes it back when she hears me come in. Her eyes scan over me and her face slowly breaks into a smile. "Now that's what I'm talking about," she grins.

Returning her smile, I perch on the edge of a chair. I still have a good fifteen minutes to wait to be picked up.

"So what's this Brett guy like then?" Rita asks. "I know you say he's the best looking man you've ever seen, but what's he like as a person?"

That's a good question. I've been working closely with him all day and for most of yesterday, but I really know very little about him. He kept the conversation firmly on work and I didn't have the guts to ask him anything about himself, although I was dying to.

"He's a little less formal than his father. I've worked for his father for three years and I still call him Mr. Connell and he's never once indicated I shouldn't. I called Brett Mr. Connell and he laughed and told me it was Brett. And yeah, that's really all I know. We've been so focused on work, on getting him caught up with where we are with everything, that there hasn't been much time to talk about anything else. I'm kind of hoping he relaxes a little tonight and I can get to know a little more about him."

"You know sometimes when a man plays it all mysterious, it's because there's really nothing to tell." Rita grins, her green eyes twinkling mischievously. "Sometimes, they're just that boring."

"Oh trust me, I know that only too well." I wince.

Rita and I giggle as we both remember Bobby, a guy I dated a year or so ago. He was the strong silent type, and I dreamed up all of these scenarios for him, and when he finally let his guard down and told me about himself, I realized he was the most boring guy I had ever met. He had a collection of train memorabilia for goodness sake.

"I don't get that impression from Brett though," I go on, aware that my voice has a dreamy quality to it that I can't quite shake. I know Rita has noticed it too by the amused smile she gives me. But I don't say anything about it, I just go on with my explanation, "I mean yeah, maybe he's secretly got a stamp collection or something, but I get the impression he's reserved around me because I work for his father. I don't know what's gone on with the family, but Brett and Mr. Connell are really formal and awkward around each other. And last year when he came into the office, they had some sort of argument where Brett thought his father had done something to make his deal fall through. He said he thought his father was trying to force him to work for the company. There's definitely some bad blood there. And I have no idea where he's been for the last year."

"Maybe he's a spy." Rita grins.

I roll my eyes.

She laughs. "Ok, seriously, he's probably not a spy. But yeah, I guess it makes sense he would be guarded around you if he has issues with his dad and he thinks you're going to run to him with anything he tells you." She laughs again. "Although I think it's fair to say his father finally got what he wanted. If only he had thought of having a heart attack sooner, you could have gotten to know the mysterious Brett before they had this falling out."

"Rita," I gasp shocked.

"Oh relax Opal, it's not like he died or anything..." She pauses for a moment and then she starts to talk again, "Ok, new scenario. Maybe he didn't disappear at all. You seem to think he's been somewhere for the last year. Maybe he just doesn't feel the need to contact his father at work. I mean when was the last time you called your dad at work?"

"Ok, fair point," I say. "But as Mr. Connell's personal assistant, I see his private diary as well and I've never once seen anything in there about him meeting up with Brett at any point over the last year either."

"So they don't get on, so they don't spend time together." Rita shrugs. "It still doesn't mean Brett's been gone for a year."

"Yeah, I guess you're right." I don't know how to explain to her that if they're running similar businesses in the same city, they would have crossed paths at some point.

"You're not convinced are you?" Rita pushes herself up into a sitting position and peering at me through narrowed eyes. "Ok, where do you think he was? Do you think he has a secret wife and kids somewhere?"

"No!" I exclaim. I hadn't even considered that as a possibility. But now I do. Am I going to go to this event tonight and end up meeting a wife I didn't know Brett had? I mean it would make sense. He's so hot it's almost impossible to imagine him not having a wife, or at least a girlfriend. But no, he can't have. Jessie would have known. She knows everything about everyone and there's no way, she wouldn't have mentioned something as big as a wife.

I open my mouth to say more, but at that moment, the buzzer on the door rings.

Rita grins at me. "Go get him," she says.

"It's not like that Rita," I insist. "It's just a work thing. Yes, I think he's attractive, but nothing will happen, even if he wanted it to. It's not professional. I just like the idea of having someone pretty to look at. It will make this dinner party a bit more interesting that's all."

"Ok hon, you keep telling yourself that." Rita smirks. "Now go."

Jumping to my feet, I hurry towards the door. I pause and look back, ready to ask Rita if I really look alright.

She grins. "You look beautiful," she says, answering my question before I even have a chance to ask it.

I smile at her and rush out of the apartment before I let my nerves get the better of me altogether. I take the stairs. It's only one floor and the stairs are usually quicker than waiting for the elevator, even in these heels. I reach the ground floor and take a deep breath then smooth my dress over my hips.

I step out into the night. A light breeze blows, bringing a chill to my bare arms and I wonder briefly if I should have worn a jacket, but I instantly dismiss the idea. It would have ruined my look, and besides, it's not like I'm going to be outside for long.

A black Mercedes is parked at the curb and a man in a black uniform stands beside it. He smiles as I approach him. "Ms Collins?" he says.

Smiling back, I give him a nod.

"Good evening," he says, pulling the back door of the car open.

"Thank you." I get into the car, trying to hide my disappointment. When Brett told me a car would pick me up at eight, for some reason, I assumed he would be in the car. I'm annoyed at myself for the misunderstanding, but I am even more annoyed at myself for being disappointed that he isn't here. If I had been coming here with Mr. Connell, I never would have expected him to be in the car he sent for me, and I certainly wouldn't have been disappointed about it. Rita is right. I am thinking about this night as way more than I should.

The driver gets into the car and starts the engine. We pull away from the curb and join the steady flow of traffic moving towards the city center.

I sit back in my seat and stare out of the window without really seeing anything. I give myself a good talking to. Yes, Brett is good looking. But I have been around good looking men before and never have I lost my mind like this. I need to get a grip of myself and fast. This is business, nothing more and nothing less and I need to remember that.

The moving scenery gets my attention as the driver pulls off the main through road and goes down a series of smaller streets. After a few moments and several more twists and turns, we're heading down a deserted country road. I remember Mr. Connell telling me that this dinner party would be held at William Hardy's home, a country mansion in the middle of nowhere.

I feel excitement swirling through my stomach again, and this time, it has nothing to do with Brett. It's a genuine excitement for the event we're going to be attending. I think it sounds like the perfect place for a nice evening of chatting and good food.

The car moves along the deserted road. Trees line the road on either side and it's so dark here that it feels like the dead of night. I imagine owls swooping through the trees and night creatures stalking through the woods. I almost laugh out loud at my own crazy thoughts, but I hold it in. I don't want Mr. Connell's driver to think I've lost the plot.

The car slows down and I peer between the seats, so I can see through the windscreen. We're approaching a large set of wrought iron gates set into a high brick wall. It looks more like a prison than a mansion, but I was expecting some sort of security to be in place. William is a multi millionaire, so he's not going to have his property open for just anyone to waltz into.

"Ms Collins representing Asima Asset Management," the driver says into the intercom.

I feel another prickle of excitement go through me. He makes it sound like I'm here as an equal to Brett, rather than as his subordinate, and I suppose in some ways, I am. I mean I know more about the company than he does certainly, and Mr. Connell himself asked me to come this evening to make sure it all goes well. To insure that Brett talks to the right people. For tonight only, maybe I can really be more than just a personal assistant. I already bring real value to the company, and maybe I can make myself even more of an asset.

The gates open and we drive through them. They begin to close the second we're inside. The long driveway is lined with manicured trees and little lights are scattered through them in strategic places, casting an ethereal glow over the road.

Yes, I say to myself, tonight is going to be a raging success, and I'm going to remind Mr. Connell of why he trusts me so much. There's going to be no flirting with Brett, no imagining what it would be like to kiss him. It's going to be all about the business.

4

We drive for what feels like at least a mile before the road before us opens out into a wide circle in front of the mansion. The mansion is beautiful, large and white and gleaming. A set of white marble stairs lead up to the doors of the house and the doors stand open and two men stand either side of them, waiters holding trays of champagne flutes. In the center of the circular road, a large fountain throws white water into the air and then the water comes cascading back down through a series of lights that makes it look like something out of a fairy tale. William has definitely gone all out on this dinner party if this is anything to go by.

I wonder for a second where all of the other cars are.

Then my question is answered when a man in black trousers and a red jacket steps out of the trees and comes to the car as it rolls to a stop at the base of the stairs. The driver rolls the window down and the man introduces himself as Mr. Hardy's valet. The driver politely declines his services, explaining that he won't be staying, he's just dropping me off. The valet nods and blends back into the shadows.

It always amazes me how the staff at these kinds of events so effortlessly fade into the background and then magically appear when they are needed.

I thank my driver and then I reach for the door handle, but before I can open the door, it opens for me and a hand reaches in. I take the hand and step out of the car, careful not to flash too much flesh as I get out. I manage to leave the car reasonably gracefully, which I'm pleased about, particularly when I look up and see the owner of the hand is Brett.

He looks as hot as always, dressed in a full black tuxedo and a crisp looking white shirt. "You look great Opal." He smiles as he releases my hand.

"Thank you," I say, feeling myself blushing slightly under his approving gaze. "You scrub up pretty well yourself."

He laughs softly and offers me his arm. "Shall we?"

Nodding at him, I link my arm through his, steeling myself for the pulse of energy that floods from him into me. I try to remind myself of the little speech I just gave myself in the car, the one where work is the only important thing tonight and I'm not going to let Brett distract me from proving my worth as an employee of Asima Asset Management. It feels like a distant memory, a promise I made in a different life, to a different version of myself.

"I must apologize for not collecting you myself Opal. I know my father would have sent a car, but I would have liked to have been a little more personal," he says.

He doesn't offer any further explanation and I can't help but think of him with his wife, too busy to worry about something as insignificant as me. "It's fine," I say. "I'm sure you were busy. Is your wife here with you tonight?"

I cringe at my blunt question. *Jeez Opal, nice going. So smooth.*

Brett laughs and shakes his head. "I'm not married."

I mutter something in response, too embarrassed to say anything else. I am elated to learn there is no wife though. Not that it matters. It doesn't change the fact that he's my boss. It doesn't magically make him available to me, or magically make him like me.

He still doesn't offer any further explanation for where he was or what he was doing instead of coming to collect me himself, and his secrecy only adds to his intrigue.

I chastise myself again. It's not secrecy. It's just none of my business what he was doing and he obviously doesn't feel the need to explain to me.

Allowing Brett to lead me to the stairs, I reach down and lift the front of my dress slightly as we climb them, not wanting my entrance to the grand building to involve me tripping and falling.

We reach the top of the stairs without incident.

Two waiters at the top of the staircase greet us and offer us champagne.

I decline. I want to get my bearings before I have a glass to contend with. My hand is shaking so much right now from the close proximity of my body to Brett's that I'm not confident I could hold it without champagne sloshing it out of the glass. Brett declines too, although I'm almost certain it's not because of any effect I might be having on him.

We step into the mansion and I am momentarily shocked into awed silence. The grand entryway is large and airy, lit by soft downlights that cast delicate shadows over everything. The space is dominated by a white marble staircase sweeping up to a walkway that runs around the entire section of the entrance way, adorned by a white decorative railing. Soft music fills the air and just below it, I can hear the humming of voices talking in polite, hushed tones.

A man appears seemingly out of nowhere.

I manage to focus on him and smile.

He returns my smile. "This way please." He turns and walks across the entryway.

We dutifully follow him while I'm wondering if I should unhook my hand from Brett's arm now.

But he keeps his arm pressed against his body, holding my hand firmly in place. I glance up at him as we walk. He looks down at me, nodding towards the man.

I realize he's the Hardy's butler.

Brett rolls his eyes and grins at me

Finally relaxing a little, I giggle softly.

Brett is probably more accustomed to this kind of setting than I am, and I like the fact that he still finds all of the pomp and circumstance mildly ridiculous. I mean who needs a butler when they have security gates in place? Surely, it's easy enough to answer your own front door. I decide to withhold my judgement. Maybe William has employed the man just for the party so he can spend his time with his guests.

The butler stops in front of a set of double doors. He bows and gestures for us to enter.

The doors are already open and even before I step in, I can see the large grand piano in the corner of the tastefully decorated room. White leather sofas line the walls, clearly pushed back to make a dance floor for later on. The floor is hard wood, and my heels clack slightly as I walk onto it.

The room already contains around two dozen people. They mill around in small groups in the center of the floor, holding wine glasses and making polite small talk. A few people sit on the couches, but most of them stand, wanting to see and be seen.

I remove my hand from Brett's arm. I miss the contact almost instantly, but I'm also relieved that I can finally breathe normally again and that my stomach isn't clenching from his touch.

A waiter approaches us with a tray of white and red wine.

I take a glass of the white wine and smile and thank him.

Brett declines a drink.

I raise an eyebrow. I hope he isn't one of those bosses that thinks even a few glasses of wine is inappropriate at a work function, because I feel like a few glasses of wine might be the only thing that'll get me through tonight without me making a total fool of myself and clamming up at the wrong moments.

A man in a very expensive looking suit is moving towards us. It is William Hardy. Beside him moves a woman who looks like she's just stepped off a magazine cover. Her hair is perfectly styled and her red dress is exquisite.

I've never met her, but I assume from the fact that William's hand is on the small of her back, guiding her forwards, that she's Tanya Hardy, William's wife.

"Opal, it's good to see you." William leans in and kisses my cheek.

"How are you?" I smile.

"Good," he responds. "How's Robert?"

It takes me half a second to realize he's talking about Mr. Connell. "He's on the mend," I say. I gesture to Brett. "This is Mr. Connell's son, Brett. He's running the company until Mr. Connell is ready to come back to work. Brett, this is William Hardy. He's been with us for a lot of years and he's one of our best clients."

Brett extends his hand to the man.

William shakes it. He winks at me. "I bet you say that about all of your clients," he says.

"Ah, only the ones I like," I joke.

He laughs and gestures to the woman in red. "This is my wife, Tanya."

We greet Tanya.

She smiles shyly which is a little surprising. She looks like the sort of woman who owns any room she steps into.

"You have a beautiful home, Tanya," I say.

"Thank you." She smiles. "I'm an interior designer and it's all my own work."

"Wow, really?" I say.

She nods her head and blushes a little.

"Honey?" William says to her. "The Jensons have just arrived." He turns to me and Brett. "Please excuse us," he says. "We'll catch up later on ok?"

I smile and nod. Tanya smiles shyly again and the pair move away.

"She isn't what I was expecting," I say to Brett. "I've never met her before, but I always thought she would be like William. Kind of loud you know? I didn't expect her to be so shy."

"She's probably not used to getting a word in, if William is the loud one." Brett grins. "And at a party like this, she's probably under strict instructions to look pretty and not steal his thunder."

I can't help but laugh. He might just be right about that. I look around the room as we talk and I spot three of the different prospects Mr. Connell has been courting. I point them out to Brett and give him some background information on each of them.

He listens attentively and nods his head.

As I'm almost finished telling him about the last potential client, a large man spots us and starts making his way towards us. He grins, a warm, friendly grin and I feel a pit of dread in my stomach. I have no idea who he is, but clearly he knows me. How could I have forgotten a client so completely that I don't recognize his face at all?

It's only when I glance at Brett and see him grinning too while stepping towards the man, do I realize with relief that it's Brett he recognizes, not me.

He reaches us and shakes Brett's hand warmly, then pulls him into a hug. "How are you?" he asks, holding Brett at arm's length for a moment and looking him up and down. He goes on without giving Brett a chance to respond, "I didn't know you were back in the city. And if I had have known, I still would never have guessed you'd be at a party like this."

"That makes two of us." Brett's grin fades a little. "I only got back to the city yesterday. My father had a heart attack and I'm overseeing his company for a couple of weeks until he's back on his feet."

"Oh shit, I'm so sorry. I've put my foot right in it haven't I," the man says, suddenly looking awkward.

"No, honestly, it's fine," Brett insists. "My father is all right. He just has to rest for a couple of weeks."

The man nods. He half turns away for a moment, scanning the room. His eyes land on a woman wearing a yellow knee length dress. "Judy," he shouts. She looks over and he beckons to her. "Come on over here. Brett's here and he's all grown up."

I smile to myself as the woman comes over.

She grabs Brett by his upper arms and kisses first one cheek and then the other. She laughs and rubs away the lipstick marks she's left. "Well, if it isn't little Brett Connell. Mind you, you're not so little now. I think you were around eleven or twelve the last time I saw you," she exclaims.

"How are you Mrs. Simmons?" Brett asks.

It's strange hearing him address the woman as Mrs. Simmons rather than using her first name, but from the short exchange they've had, I'm guessing the couple are old friends of the Connells and Brett probably grew up addressing the couple as Mr. and Mrs. Simmons because of his father's insistence on everything being formal and proper.

"Oh, I'm good thank you," Mrs. Simmons says. "And how about you? What are you doing with yourself these days?"

"Well, I'm currently sitting in for my father for a few weeks," Brett says, carefully skipping over the part about the heart attack, not wanting to make the same mistake as he made with Mr. Simmons and making everything awkward. "But I have my own company now. I've actually been in France for the last year overseeing the opening of a new branch out there."

He's been in France. That explains why I haven't seen him in a year. So from the argument I overheard with him and his father, it seems like Mr. Connell tried to do something to stop Brett from expanding his business overseas.

"Oh, how exciting!" Mrs. Simmons gushes. "I love France."

"Me too," Mr. Simmons puts in. "There's a hell of a market for asset management over there right now. And of course, it doesn't hurt that it's such a romantic place right? Not for a young guy like you."

I get the impression he added that last bit for his wife's benefit.

Brett looks kind of awkward and he just smiles.

"So?" Mr. Simmons presses him. "Have you met any nice girls out there? Anyone special?"

Brett shakes his head.

I sigh with relief. No wife. No significant other. Not that it should matter to me. But it does. No matter how much I try to tell myself nothing can happen between Brett and I, and that he has shown no signs whatsoever that he's even interested in me, hearing that he's not taken still makes me feel good.

My sigh draws their attention to me.

I feel myself blush when all of their eyes land on me at once.

"Where are my manners?" Brett says. "Opal, this is Mr. and Mrs. Simmons, old friends of my parents."

"Less of the old," Mr. Simmons says, shaking my hand.

"Mr. and Mrs. Simmons, this is Opal Collins. She's my father's personal assistant and she's helping me settle into the company."

"Oh, you're Opal," Mrs. Simmons says, nodding to me. "Robert speaks very highly of you."

Smiling, I am flattered that Mr. Connell has said nice things about me. I am a little disappointed that the introductions seem to have brought the original conversation to a halt though. I was learning more about Brett.

"What's it like working for Robert then?" Mr. Simmons winks at me. "Tell me everything. All of the things I can use against him, especially."

I start to tell him about my job and what it's like to work for the company. Naturally, I don't tell him anything bad, although in fairness, I really enjoy my job, and it would be hard for me to think of anything particularly bad to say about working for Mr. Connell or the company.

Brett is talking animatedly to Mrs. Simmons and I try to listen, but Mr. Simmons won't give me a chance to pause to see what I can hear. He fires question after question at me, and in the end, I give up trying to hear anything interesting about Brett's life. I do notice though that when a waiter comes by, myself and the Simmons' switch our empty glasses for fresh ones, that Brett takes one too. Good. Maybe he will loosen up a little after all.

After what feels like forever, the Simmons' excuse themselves and move on to talk to another couple that stand nearby.

"I'm sorry about that," Brett says.

I frown. "Sorry about what?"

"Mr. Simmons. He's harmless enough, but he's a little full on isn't he?"

"He sure likes to ask a lot of questions," I say, going for the answer I hope is tactful.

"He's always been the same," Brett says.

Before I can say anything else, we are approached again. This time, it's by one of Mr. Connell's potential leads. I nudge Brett, hoping he'll remember who the man is.

Brett doesn't disappoint and he launches into a speech about the company and what they can do for the man. I throw in a supporting point here and there, and by the end of the conversation, Brett has a meeting organized with him.

Over the course of the next hour, that pattern repeats itself time and time again. Brett and I find ourselves momentarily alone and we just start to speak to each other when we are interrupted again. Each time, it's like we're starting over and we never get a chance to move past the small talk and talk about anything outside of work stuff. The more times we get interrupted, the more I can feel myself getting annoyed at everyone who approaches us. I want to scream at them to go away and leave us alone for ten minutes.

The wine is flowing and people are starting to relax more, so the constant stream of people wanting to talk to Brett and me is only getting longer and more annoying. I'm debating excusing myself to go to the bathroom to try to get a handle on how frustrated the constant interruptions are making me, when I hear a clinking sound.

I look in the direction of the door we entered through where the sound is coming from.

William and Tanya stand in the doorway.

William is tapping something against a glass. He waits until he has the attention of the room. "Ladies and gentleman, dinner is about to be served. Please follow us to the dining room." He turns and moves away.

Then as one, the guests begin to follow him. He leads us across the entrance way and through a door on the opposite side of the mansion. The dining room is huge, and a long table in the center of the room is set for dinner.

People make their way towards the table and I follow Brett as he moves towards one of the ends. A woman in a white dress with a long string of pearls around her neck moves in on Brett's other side.

It becomes instantly clear to me that she's moved in on purpose, planning to sit beside him for the dinner, and maybe try to get her claws into him.

I feel a surge of jealousy, but it fades slightly when Brett catches my eye and eye rolls in the woman's direction and then pulls a face. I grin at him and he laughs softly. We reach the table and Brett pulls out a chair for me. I thank him and he nods then takes the seat beside me.

Pearl woman pounces on the seat on the other side of Brett and promptly engages him in conversation.

I can't hear what she's saying. I think she's purposely keeping her voice low, trying to freeze me out of the conversation, and much to my dismay, it seems to be working. Brett nods along with her, smiling politely and occasionally answering her questions. He doesn't seem particularly interested in what she's saying, but he doesn't seem to be attempting to shut her up, so he can turn back and talk to me either.

I sit awkwardly, not sure where to look as Brett ignores me on one side of me, and the man at my other side talks to the woman beside him, presumably his wife. I pick up my glass and drink some wine, more for something to focus on than anything else.

After a few painful minutes, the doors from the kitchen open as a team of waiters and waitresses stream in, each carrying two plates. They position themselves around the table, and then as one, they place a plate before each guest.

Staring down at the plate, I'm overjoyed to see the starter is a prawn cocktail, one of my favorites. As I reach for my fork, my arm brushes against Brett's and I look up. He's finally facing towards me, ready to talk to me. Part of me wants to be short with him and tell him not to bother, but I remind myself this is a business event, not a date, and he's under no obligation to focus on me all night.

"I'm sorry about that," he says quietly, leaning in so no one else can hear our conversation. "She's the wife of one of my clients and she seems to have taken a liking to me. I have to walk a very fine line between being attentive enough not to upset her and have husband fire me and no so attentive that I give her even the slightest hint that I'm interested in her. Which I'm not."

I feel slightly better about being ignored since he's explained the situation. I know exactly where he's coming from. There's always that one client or client's partner that needs to be made to feel special. I also couldn't help but notice he made a point of letting me know he wasn't interested in her. I want to read something into this, but the rational side of me won't let me read anything into it. It was just the fact he didn't want me to think he was pursuing a client's wife.

We finish our starters and the team of wait staff clear the table quickly and efficiently and bring out our main courses. The main course is a beautifully presented chicken breast wrapped in flaky pastry and stuffed with cheese and pancetta. It is served with a medley of roasted vegetables and creamy looking mashed potato. I cut into the chicken and chew it slowly, relishing the flavor. It is cooked to perfection, moist, juicy and utterly delicious.

"So are you having a good time?" Brett asks me.

I smile and nod. "Yes. It's fascinating to see how other people live isn't it?" I say. "Although I must admit I was starting to find it overwhelming keeping track of everyone earlier. Don't worry though, I have the important people to the company memorized."

"Relax Opal." Brett laughs. "It wasn't a test. I was just making sure you were enjoying the evening. I know what a drag it can be when you have to attend these things regularly and I wanted to make sure you weren't too bored."

I laugh softly with him and shake my head. "I'm definitely not bored," I say. "And to be honest, it's very rare I come to these things. Your father usually comes alone or brings your mother. I only step in when he can't attend for some reason."

"Ah, so it's all still fairly new to you then," Brett says. "Don't worry, you'll start to dread them soon enough."

"So you were dreading this evening?" I ask.

"Actually, I thought this evening might be a bit more entertaining than normal. You know, because I thought it would be nice to get to know you a little better, outside of the office."

My heart skips a beat. Did he really just say what I thought he said? He did. I know he did. He didn't mean it in the way I wish he meant it, but it's good to know he's at least willing to give us a chance to be more than formal colleagues.

"I'm sorry, was that crossing a line?" Brett frowns.

I realize I have been quiet too long, stunned into blissful silence by his revelation. I shake my head. "No. Not at all," I say quickly. "I was just a little surprised by it, that's all. I've worked for your father for three years now, almost a year as his personal assistant, and he's never once made an effort to get to know me as a person."

"Yeah, he's old school," Brett says, waving his hand dismissively. "He still thinks there should be a professional distance between employees and their boss."

"And what do you think about that?" I ask, the wine and Brett's sudden friendliness making me brave.

"I think people generally work better together when they know each other socially. I think it's good to get to know the people I work alongside. There's a time and a place to be formal, but there's also a time and a place to be something a little more."

I can't decide if he's flirting with me or not. I don't think he is. I'm sure if he were, he would be a lot better at it, leaving me in no doubt about it. But I so badly want him to be flirting with me that I allow myself to believe that maybe he's testing the water a little bit to see if I would respond if he did so. "I agree," I say. "I don't think there's any harm in people getting to know each other, outside of the office." My cheeks flush as I speak. I quickly pick up my wine glass and take a drink so I can look anywhere but at Brett's intense, probing eyes.

"So tell me something about you," he says. "Something that you wouldn't bring up at the office."

As I set my glass down, I wrack my brains trying to come up with something mildly interesting. When I'm put on the spot this way, I realize how boring my life is. How normal and run of the mill I am. It's like when someone asks what my hobbies are. I'd love to be able to say white water rafting, or parachute jumping or something interesting, instead of reading and watching movies. "I was once the captain of the girl's football team when I was in school."

"Really?" Brett tilts his head at me. "And did you guys win anything?"

"Not that I remember."

"You wouldn't remember if you had?" he says, raising an eyebrow.

"Probably not. We were six at the time."

Brett throws his head back and laughs.

"What about you?" I say, feeling brave again, since he's laughing. "Tell me something about you." *Please don't say you're a train spotter or that you collect anything vaguely train related.*

"On my gap year, which my father wasn't at all happy about me having, I backpacked extensively and I climbed Kilimanjaro."

"Wow, really? That makes my football thing seem a little tame," I say.

"But is it true? Your football story?" he asks.

"Of course." I frown.

"Then your story is better than mine." He grins. "Because mine isn't technically true. I did go backpacking and I did plan to climb Kilimanjaro, but I twisted my ankle getting off the coach before we started to climb it."

"No way!" I laugh.

"Yes way," he says laughing with me. "My buddies went ahead and climbed the mountain, while I was taken to a local hospital just to make sure I hadn't broken any bones."

"At least, I made it onto the pitch." I laugh. I'm dying to ask him about France, but I'm afraid if I do, he'll think I'm trying to steer the conversation back to work and so instead, I ask him about his time back packing.

"We went across Europe and then we went through Russia and across most of Asia," he says. "What about you? Have you travelled much?"

"Not really. I've been on a few girly vacations to Spain and I've done city breaks here and there, but I never did the gap year thing. I'd like to travel more one day though. Where would you recommend?"

"It depends on what you're looking for," Brett says. "I really enjoyed India, but I know it's not for everyone. Vietnam was great for culture and history and you can't beat Italy for a good touristy spot mixed in with culture too."

"I've always fancied Rome," I say.

"It's a beautiful city. I'd like to go back there one day. Especially now, since I'm a bit older and I might appreciate the sights a little more rather than spending most of my time in bars."

I bite my tongue to stop myself just in time before I blurt out that we should go there together one day. Hell, what am I thinking? I'm letting my guard down way too far. I am losing it.

6

I'm glad for the interruption when the wait staff comes back again and clears away the remains of the main course, replacing it with a watermelon and kiwi fruit flavored mousse, decorated with an intricate sugar basket. "I can make these," I say, nodding to the sugar basket.

"You should have led with that instead of the football story. Everyone loves someone who can make a mean dessert." Brett laughs.

"If you think that's impressive, you should try my chocolate chip cookies," I joke.

"Don't make jokes like that Opal. It's just mean unless you plan on bringing a batch to the office one day." Brett smiles.

"Oh, you never know, I just might do that," I respond with a grin, glad we've moved on to a slightly less dangerous subject.

"I'm holding you to that," Brett says.

Nodding, I smile again. It's nice to chat to Brett in a more relaxed setting. I'm still totally enthralled by him and I still find my mind wandering to a place where he's holding me in his arms, kissing me passionately, but it's nice to see a less formal side to him. He's smiling, laughing and sharing little things about his life with me. It's nothing particularly meaningful, but still, it's nice to see the man behind the corporate face a little bit.

As I listen to him telling me a story about a time at college when he and some of his friends where the victims of a rather embarrassing prank, I realize something. When Brett isn't focused on work so much, not only is he smoking hot, but he's also much more likeable as a person. When he's smiling, laughing and talking to me this way, I don't feel like he's so much of an enigma. I feel like I could actually get past the cold corporate face and get to know him a bit.

Or maybe a lot.

I'm not sure if that's a good thing or a bad thing. While I am most definitely enjoying his company, it's dangerous, because finding out he's funny and charming beneath the cool veneer he presents at work is only making me like him even more. And that's bound to lead to me getting hurt.

"So basically, the night ended with me and three other guys stark naked and locked out of the dorms," Brett says.

I realize I have missed most of his story as my mind wandered, but just that line alone is enough to give me the gist of it…I laugh and shake my head.

"What did you do?" I ask.

"We spent a very cold and uncomfortable night hiding out in a nearby shed." Brett snickers. "And the next morning, we waited for someone to leave the dorms so we could slip inside. It must have been quite a sight for that poor guy. There he is, minding his own business, going for a run, when four naked guys rush past him and dart up the stairs."

I giggle, picturing the scene. "I hope you got your own back."

"Oh, we did," Brett says. "Believe me, we did. We basically spent the rest of the year goofing around and pranking each other. As I'm sure you can imagine, my parents weren't in the least bit impressed with my grades that year. But in the end, I buckled down and got my degree. Not because I wanted my father's approval, but because I started to think seriously about what I would do after college. I knew my father wanted me to go and work for him, and I didn't want to. I guess I realized that if I failed at school, I wouldn't have many other options."

"So your father paid for a fancy degree, so you'd go work for him and instead, that motivated you to not work for him?"

"Yup. Ironic huh?" Brett nodded.

"Indeed." I smile. "But I have to ask. Why was the thought of working for your father so unbearable?"

"I guess because all of my life, it had just been assumed that's what I would do. I started to feel trapped and I realized that my parents' dream wasn't the same as mine. I wanted to do something just for me, to prove to myself that I could make it on my own, without having to ride on my father's name. Stupid huh?"

"Not at all! I get it. It must have been hard to walk away though." I stared at him.

"In some ways it was, but in other ways, it was a relief. Anyway, enough about that. It's getting awfully close to being work talk isn't it?"

"Yeah a little," I agree, although I still have a hundred questions I want to ask him about it.

I reach for my wine. The glass had been consistently topped up throughout the evening's meal and I'm starting to feel a little tipsy. But I'm enjoying the conversation and the giddy feeling, so I keep drinking, even though I know I really should stop.

Gazing around after I've taken a drink, I see that most of the other guests have left the table and wandered back through to the piano room. "Should we go back through to the other room?"

Brett nods somewhat reluctantly.

I feel my heart slam in my chest. Was he enjoying being almost alone with me, or is it just that he knows once we're back in the other room, he's going to have to get back into work mode and schmooze a few more leads?

He stands.

I follow him, feeling slightly unsteady on my feet, but not enough so just anyone would notice. We go back into the piano room. The soft music has been replaced with something a bit more livelily and several people are dancing.

Brett looks at me and raises an eyebrow.

I laugh softly. I guess I'm not the only one who has overindulged on the wine slightly.

Brett nods to an empty spot on one of the couches. "Do you want to sit down or have you worn your dancing shoes?"

"Let's just sit down for now," I say.

"Oh, thank God!" He grins. "I was almost afraid you'd choose dancing and see my two left feet in action." He leads me to the empty spot on the couch.

Within seconds, a potential client has approached us and he and Brett fall into a deep conversation about solutions and investments. Once I'm confident Brett has a handle on the conversation, I switch off from it, looking around at the other people in the room.

We're not the only ones huddled down no doubt making deals, but I suddenly find myself wishing I'd chosen dancing, even though I know my feet would have been killing me by now. The people who are just treating tonight as a party seem to be having so much more fun than the people sitting talking. But I remind myself I'm not here for a party. I'm here as a representative of Asima Asset Management and I'm here to get new clients, not have a good time.

Brett shifts slightly beside me.

I glance at him out of the corner of my eye as his thigh brushes up against mine. He doesn't seem to have noticed our thighs are now touching, but holy shit I've noticed. My thigh is warm where it touches his, sparks flowing from the spot and running through my whole body.

I feel my pussy clench as I look at him, trying and failing to ignore the touch of his thigh, trying and failing to not think about how I want to feel him inside of me. I can't help letting myself imagine pushing my hands into his hair and slowly stripping him down. I imagine his hands all over my body, working me into a frenzy, until finally, he makes love to me for hours.

With a start, I discover that my pussy is getting wet just thinking about it and I'm suddenly flustered. I'm in a room full of people, many of them associates or clients and I am practically coming in my panties. I know I'm wearing a stupid smile on my face, and I can feel that my skin is flushed, not just on my face, but all down my neck and across my chest too. God, how could I forget myself like this? I'm really not safe to be allowed around Brett, especially when there's wine on the go.

I touch Brett's arm, feeling my pussy clenching again, as my skin brushes over his suit jacket, feeling the taut muscles beneath it.

He looks up at me, a questioning look on his face.

I note that my hand is still sitting on his arm and I pull it away quickly, hoping he hasn't noticed the weird moment between us. His slight frown tells me he has noticed, and I'm suddenly glad of the potential client still being there beside him. He can hardly ask me about it with a potential client in ear shot.

"Would you excuse me for just a moment please?" I say in a breathy voice, forcing myself to smile like everything is completely normal between us.

"Sure." Brett nods giving me a quick, unsure looking smile that's different from his normal.

I want to say more, but I can't, not with the potential client sitting there. I tell myself that's a good thing. I would only end up blurting out something embarrassing which I would hastily come to regret.

It doesn't matter anyway. Even if I had something else to say, something I could say in public, I couldn't get it in now without looking rude as Brett turns straight back to the conversation he's in. I guess it's a good thing that at least one of us still has our head in the game. It doesn't feel like a good thing though and I suddenly wish I hadn't asked him if he wanted to come back through here. It was so much nicer at the dining table, locked in a conversation between just the two of us. Mr. Connell wouldn't be too happy to learn that we dropped the ball at this party though.

Despite all of that, I still feel a pang of jealousy going through me again at the potential client who holds Brett's attention in a way I can only dream of.

Realizing I have sat for too long after asking to be excused, I get to my feet to stumble through the crowd and find the bathroom. God, what am I doing? How have I let Brett get so far under my skin so quickly?

I use the toilet and go to the sink to wash my hands. I leave my hands under the cool water for a moment until I feel like I have myself back under some sort of control. I have to get a grip of myself and start acting like a professional, instead of some love sick teenager. Ideally, before Brett notices I'm acting oddly.

It's probably already too late for that, but if I can find a way to start acting like my normal self again, then hopefully Brett will think he just imagined the strange moment between us where our thighs were pressed together and my hand lingered on his arm for just a little too long.

7

I've been standing here in the bathroom trying to talk some sense into myself for far too long and now I'm too nervous to come back out. How am I going to explain to Brett why I've been in here for almost ten minutes? He's probably going to think I've been throwing up or something after the amount of wine he's seen me guzzling. It's really not an image I want him having in his mind when he thinks of me.

I can't just stay in here all night though. The longer I spend in here agonizing over coming back out, the longer I'll be missing and the worse it'll be when I finally do go back to Brett. Inspiration comes to me and the answer is so obvious I give out a soft laugh. I'll just say I ran into someone I knew and I was talking to them.

God, I'm losing my actual fucking mind here. As if I couldn't think of that sooner. What the hell is wrong with me? Is it the wine? Brett's effect on me? Both of those things? It's most likely a combination of both.

I swiftly dry my hands and step out of the bathroom. I shake my head at myself and my own paranoia. The party is in full swing now with more people up dancing and those sitting around seem to be laughing and having a good time now, rather than talking business quite so much. So no one will have even noticed how long I've been gone. Especially not Brett. And even if he has noticed, it isn't as if he's going to care. He's only here with me because he has no choice. It's not like he would have chosen to bring me.

This thought should make me feel better, but instead, it gives me a twisty, crampy feeling in my stomach. As much as it pains me to admit it, I want him to have noticed. To have noticed and maybe even be a little bit worried about me.

Damnit Opal, get a grip of yourself. You're not fifteen. Stop acting like you are.

I'm almost back at the piano room when I feel my purse vibrating. I stop to open it and pull my phone out. I'm getting a call from an unknown number. I rarely answer my personal phone to numbers I don't know and I go to push my phone back into my purse when I change my mind. It could be Mr. Connell calling from the hospital. It makes sense that he would call if he's awake to see how the dinner party is going and to check in and see if we're getting anywhere with the leads.

Mr. Connell will be angry with me if I ignore his call...if I don't answer, he might call Brett instead. "Hello," I say as I take the call.

I can hear a male voice, obviously I was right and the call is from Mr. Connell, but the music is too loud for me to make out the words. I'm just glad I took the call. "I can't hear you properly. Hang on a moment please," I say, hoping he can hear me.

Looking around for a quieter spot, I see a pair of double glass doors pushed open letting in some fresh air. I move over to the doors and peer outside. The doors lead to a pretty patio area, decked out in sandy colored wood and decorated with an array of small bushes and flowers in pots. The area is encased with a decorative wooden fence and a little gate leads out and down into the main gardens.

Moving away from the house, I head to the small fence, resting my elbows on it and looking out into the garden. I can still hear the music drifting on the air, but it's quiet now, like I can hear it in the distance. I bring my phone back up to my ear. "I'm sorry Mr. Connell. The music was rather loud inside and I couldn't hear you. What can I do for you?"

"Mr. Connell huh?" The voice is low and filled with a kind of mean amusement. I recognize that voice instantly. Gary, my ex-boyfriend. I feel my heart sink. I never should have taken the call, but it's not like I was expecting Gary to somehow have my new number.

Gary and I broke up a couple of months ago. We had been dating for a while and I was starting to think the relationship might be going somewhere, but as we spent more time together, Gary started to reveal his true colors and I found that I didn't much like the person he hid under the charming act. He would act get jealous and controlling. He didn't like me going out with my friends. He didn't even like me going to work. And he would fly into rages when I would tell him I was going out with Rita or Jessie, or doing pretty much anything that didn't involve him. He was too clingy for my liking and I knew things would only get worse if I stuck around, so I ended things between us.

Our breakup hadn't exactly been pleasant. Gary had apologized over and over again for his possessiveness, saying he was just afraid he would lose me. I almost caved, but as I opened my mouth to tell him I'd give him one more chance, I changed my mind. The truth is, I had seen I wasn't really into Gary. I didn't want to be with someone who thought it was okay to treat me that way, regardless of the reasoning behind it. I told him it was over. Afterward, he hadn't really taken no for an answer, constantly calling me, texting me, and even turning up at my apartment. He tried to say we should take a break and then try again, but I was so done with him that I didn't even entertain the idea.

I had threatened him with a restraining order the second time he turned up at the apartment and he stopped appearing there, but the calls and texts hadn't stopped. They varied between Gary begging me for a second chance, saying he loved me, and him telling me I was unattractive, fat, stupid, any of a hundred mean things, and that I might as well get back with him because no one else would ever love me.

In the end, I had changed my phone number and it had all stopped. I had really begun to believe I was free of him, but now apparently, he had found my new number. I really could have done without that happening. I had almost forgotten how annoying it was to be harassed over the phone constantly by someone.

"Gary..." I sigh into the phone. "I think I've made it clear I don't want to talk to you. How many other ways can I tell you that?"

"Don't be like that Opal. Do you have any idea how hard it's been to get this number? Surely, that tells you I'm serious about us and that I've changed."

Yeah, sure. Changed from a control freak boyfriend to a stalker ex boyfriend. Perfect.

"How did you get this number?" I ask him the question partly because it gives him something to focus on other than his obsession with me and partly because I'm genuinely curious. If someone has given it to him, then when I change it again, I know who not to give the new number to, so he doesn't get it again. I really thought I had only given it to people who could be trusted this time, but evidently not.

"It doesn't matter how I got the number. It only matters that I did. I had to find the number Opal. I had to be able to call you. I know you're mad at me still, and I get it, I do. But you have to give me a chance to prove to you that I've changed," he says.

"I don't have to do anything." I roll my eyes.

"But I love you Opal," he says.

I'm really sick of this now. I need to hang up. Gary is a weirdo who I don't need in my life, and the way he says my name with almost every sentence feels creepy and weird. I'm starting to feel the familiar panic he always drew out in me. It's like whenever I talk to Gary I feel trapped, reminded of how I felt when I was with him.

Gary must take my silence to mean he's still in with a shot. He's talking again, telling me how it will be different this time, how he will treat me like a queen, and how he understands that I need time to myself to go out with my friends.

As he babbles on, I become aware of a presence behind me and I turn slightly. I gasp in a breath as I see Brett behind me. He's so close that if I had taken a step back, I would have fallen into his arms. I didn't even hear him approaching. It's like he just materialized there out of thin air.

I give him a half smile and I find my eyes locked on his. For a delicious moment, I think he'll kiss me.

He holds my gaze and runs the tip of his tongue over his lips, but of course he doesn't kiss me, he just smiles questioningly at me. "Is everything all right?"

I nod, smiling apologetically. I realize Gary is still rambling on and suddenly, I don't care if I piss him off. I've always been careful, trying to cajole Gary into leaving me alone rather than demanding it, because I have always been afraid he would turn up at my apartment again. But right now, looking into Brett's eyes, I feel brave. "Gary? I have to go." I end the call in the middle of his protest.

"You left me in the shark tank all alone," Brett says with a half smile.

"Sorry," I say, holding up my phone before I push it back into my purse. "I thought it might have been your father."

"You really think my mom will let him make work calls from the hospital?" Brett laughs.

I laugh with him. "No, I guess not," I admit. "Especially not if she thinks he's calling me. She really hates me doesn't she?"

"No," Brett says. "She hates the fact that my father can't stop working for even a second. But I mean he'd just had a heart attack today and she could hardly be overly mad with him, so she took it out on you, that's all."

I mull over his words. It makes sense I suppose.

"Why do you care whether she likes you or not anyway?" Brett asks.

Because it will make our wedding pretty awkward if your mother hates me, I think to myself, instantly pushing the thought away. "Oh I don't care at all…I was just curious as to why."

Brett smiles back at me, a wide smile that makes his eyes sparkle and reveals a tiny dimple in his left cheek.

I instantly want to reach up and touch it. The smile changes his whole face, making him look a little less serious, like he's someone you could have actual fun with. "You know, smiling suits you. You should do it more often," I blurt out without thinking.

Brett gives a soft laugh. "Is that so? Maybe you have some other suggestions, seeing as how you haven't been able to take your eyes off me all night," he says in a low voice.

His tone sets my heart racing. I feel my cheeks burning at his words. Dammit. He wasn't supposed to notice. "I don't know what you're talking about," I say, and even to me, it sounds like the lie it is.

"Sure you do." He flashes me that wide smile again.

For a second, I allow myself to forget that he's my boss and I've just massively embarrassed myself in front of him. In fact, I forget everything except how his eyes look as he smiles. He winks at me and I feel my pussy clench.

"Do you know how I know that?" he asks. He doesn't wait for me to answer, "I know it because I haven't been able to stop watching you either, Opal."

It should be creepy to hear he's been watching me all night, but it isn't. It's brilliant, amazing and just what I wanted to hear.

Brett looks totally relaxed and confident, even as he tells me he's been watching me. He looks sexier than ever if that's even possible. His words and the wine come together inside of me to make me brave and I smile at him, a half smile that raises only one corner of my lips. "Are you saying you find me attractive?" I ask in a soft, breathy voice.

Brett doesn't answer immediately, but he looks me up and down, his eyes sweeping slowly across every inch of my body.

His hot penetrating gaze makes me feel naked. I feel the heat in my cheeks increasing, and my heart is beating so fast I think it might explode. My body is taut, primed, craving his touch.

"I think we both know the answer to that question," he says. His voice is dripping with lust, his eyes darkening, and he takes a step closer to me.

He's standing so close now that I can feel the heat emanating from his body. If I moved forward so much as an inch, I would be pressed against him.

I can see the movement in his chest as he breathes, and I can feel his breath on my face. He's breathing faster than normal and I know I am too. I so desperately want to lean in and run my tongue gently over his lips, and then press my mouth against his. I want him to wrap me in his arms and never let me go. I want to taste every inch of him, run my hands over his whole body.

"Why Mr. Connell, I do believe you're flirting with me," I say with a teasing smile.

I want so badly for him to kiss me that it's like a physical ache inside of me. I hope my words will push him over the edge and make him do it.

Instead, they have the opposite effect. He takes a step back from me, opening up a gap between us. He takes a sip of his wine and clears his throat. "I'm sorry. I don't know what came over me," he says. The playful tone is gone from his voice and his eyes no longer burn into mine. "It would be awfully unprofessional if anything were to happen between us."

Cursing myself inside, I realize I called him Mr. Connell because I thought it would sound sexy, like an Austen kind of sexy I guess. Instead, it reminded Brett that he's my boss and reminded him why he can't do this. Can't do me.

Fuck.

He takes another drink, then he turns and heads back towards the double doors.

I don't make any attempt to follow him. I'm still reeling from the closeness of his body to mine.

He reaches the doors and turns back for a moment. "For the record though, you look stunning tonight," he says with a flash of a smile, then he turns back and disappears inside of the mansion.

8

Frozen to the spot for the moment, I stare at the door where Brett disappeared as if looking at that spot will somehow clear everything up for me. I never dared imagine for even a minute that Brett might find me as intoxicatingly attractive as I find him but now he's shown me the truth, it makes me want him even more. We could enjoy each other's bodies, make each other come to life. And does it really matter if he's my boss? I mean we're both adults and it isn't like I'm thinking we should go around the office holding hands or anything. Surely, we can be professional at work and a little closer outside of work.

No one would ever have to know.

Whatever may or may not happen between Brett and I doesn't change the fact I have a job to do right now. Or the fact the night air is becoming a little chilly, and the goose bumps on my arms are no longer just from Brett standing so close to me. I move towards the double doors and back into the mansion. I go through to the piano room and I instantly spot Brett before I have even consciously looked for him. It's as though my eyes are just naturally attracted to his beauty, searching him out of their own accord.

He's talking to Mr. Simmons again, and I decide against going over there. Mr. Simmons will only start quizzing me. To be honest, I'm still so thrown by my conversation with Brett on the decking, so I'm afraid I might blurt out something I shouldn't.

Instead of heading over towards Brett and Mr. Simmons, I head towards Barney Lawson, another client of the firm who I have just spotted. I smile a greeting at him and he instantly begins chatting to me, asking me how Mr. Connell is doing and what happened. I fill him in and assure him his business is in safe hands.

"With him?" Barney says, nodding towards Brett.

"Yes," I say, a little surprised. "How did you know? Have you met Mr. Connell's son before?"

"No," Barney says, shaking his head. "I didn't even know Robert had a son. I just figured you meant him because you were looking at him when you said I would be taken care of."

"Oh," I reply stupidly. I catch myself and I know I can save this one. Barney gave me a readymade reason to be looking in Brett's direction as I spoke to him. "Yes, yes of course. Brett has actually been out of the country expanding his own business."

I can hardly say I haven't been able to take my eyes off Brett since I came back in from outside can I? Instead, I give him a snippet of information I hope is interesting enough to distract him from my obvious discomfort when he said I was looking at Brett.

It seems to work and Barney switches topics, chatting to me about his own son who is almost ready to graduate high school.

I relax into the conversation since it's on safer ground, but I still find my eyes drawn to Brett. I find it hard to maintain eye contact with Barney for more than a few seconds before I'm looking at Brett again.

I'm relieved when Barney finally excuses himself from my company. I mean he's a nice enough guy and I thought being pulled into a conversation would distract me from Brett, but it just didn't work. I can't keep my eyes off him as I find myself slipping into a daydream about Brett, where he takes me in his arms, kisses me, makes love to me.

A waiter saunters towards me and seeing my empty glass, he holds out his tray. I put my empty glass on it and replace it with a full one, smiling and thanking him. I take my glass and go to sit on one of the couches. I sit back, leaning into the soft cushions and sipping my wine. I am still watching Brett, but now I think at least it looks a little more subtle. Anyone glancing at me would just assume I was watching the guests dancing.

The rest of the night drags on as I force myself to make polite conversation with the stream of people who see me alone and approach me, thinking I am maybe in need of company. I know I look like a total sad case, but Brett is expertly working the room now and I don't want to get in the way. And truth be told, I'm not sure I trust myself to be in close proximity to him and not reach out to touch him.

As the night goes on, the first of the guests start to slowly leave and within an hour, more and more people have made their excuses and slipped away. The crowd is down to about half the amount we started with and I have put away another two glasses of wine. I'm starting to think Brett and I should be leaving soon too, but he's deep in a conversation with one of the potential clients his father has been warming up, and I know better than to interrupt that. It seems I still have a few of my wits about me. That's something, I suppose.

I finish my drink and I put the glass down on the small table beside the couch, telling myself I won't be having anymore tonight.

A waitress materialises at my side almost instantly as though my vow to not drink anymore wine has summoned her to test my resolve.

Smiling politely at her, I shake my head. "No more for me thank you."

She smiles and nods then moves on.

I turn back to where Brett is talking to the potential client, but he's gone.

"Hey," he says from beside me

He's so close that I feel his warm breath on my ear as he speaks. I jump.

He chuckles softly. "Sorry. I thought you saw me coming."

Shaking my head, I'm momentarily mute as I stare at his face. Every time I tell myself I'm prepared to see him up close and that I won't let him affect me, the universe takes it as a challenge and shows me just how much of an effect he has on me. I'm honestly quite surprised he managed to come and sit beside me while I was talking to the waitress without me noticing.

"Are you about ready to leave?" he asks.

Still mute, I nod. I have wanted to leave for a while, but I realize leaving the party means leaving Brett and I suddenly don't want this night to end. I have a feeling once it does, we'll just go back to being a boss and his personal assistant and that cool distance will be back between us.

Brett stands and offers me his hand.

I take a deep breath and slip my hand into his, waiting for the sparks I know will come. I'm not wrong. My hand tingles where it touches his and his warmth seems to spread right up my arm. I let him pull me to my feet. "There's a few people I need to say goodbye to," I say.

"Yeah me too," he agrees. "Meet me at the front door in five?"

I nod. At least he's not abandoning me completely. He can't because he will have to call my driver as I have no idea of his number, but I tell myself it's more than that. I tell myself he doesn't want this night to end either. I know I'm probably wrong, but it makes me feel warm inside, so I let myself believe it for a moment, telling myself it's harmless.

Returning to say my goodbyes to the few remaining clients and a couple of other people I know, I finally thank the host and his wife for a lovely evening. I hurry out of the piano room before anyone else can latch onto me, and make my way to the front door where Brett waits for me.

He smiles as I approach him.

Looking down, I feel my cheeks warming again as I look at him through my eyelashes and give him a shy smile. I look up properly in time to catch him staring back at me with undisguised lust on his face. I swallow hard as I feel my cheeks getting redder, but I ignore them and close the gap between Brett and I. By the time I reach his side, he has regained his composure. Shame. I really liked that look on his face, even if it did make me blush right down my neck and chest rather than just on my face.

"I've called for a car," he says. "I thought we could just share one. I hope that's okay with you?"

"Of course." It's better than okay. It means our night together can last a little bit longer.

Brett's phone beeps. He pulls it out and glances at it briefly. "That was my driver. Our car is here."

"That quickly?" I ask, surprised. I expected us to have wait at least half an hour or so.

Brett smiles and nods. "My driver doesn't go far. There's an all night diner a mile or so down the road. He'll have most likely waited there with a coffee and perhaps a burger." He holds his arm out to me.

Taking his arm, I feel kind of giddy as the sparks fly up and down my body As we step outside, I stumble slightly and find myself leaning against Brett's side.

"Are you all right?" he asks.

I look up and find him gazing down at me. His eyes have darkened again, and I know the touching of our bodies is having the same effect on him as it is on me. I can hardly breathe as I peer up at him and just nod to answer his question. I don't think I can utter a single word right now.

He moves his arm away.

I feel a second of such intense loss that I can't breathe, but his hand isn't gone from me for long, and when he puts it on the small of my back to guide me down the steps safely, I find I still can't breathe but this time, it's for a different reason.

I take the steps slowly, aware of how much I have drank, but with Brett's hand on my back, I feel like I'm floating on air and I get down the steps easily. I have never met anyone who has this effect on me before, and I don't know what exactly it is about Brett produces such a strong response in me. But I do know this—I have to have him. If I don't, I will end up absolutely crazy.

We reach the car and Brett opens the door for me. I thank him, pleased when my voice comes out sounding normal, and I get into the car.

He closes the door, goes around to the other side and gets in beside me. He asks the driver to drop me off first and we pull away. Brett sits looking out of the window.

After glancing at him a few times, hoping he will start a conversation, I give up and do the same. I can feel the tension between us. The air in the back of the car feels thick, like the sexual chemistry between us has taken on a physical form. I try my best to think of something to say to break the tension between us, but I can't think of anything.

It's only when we're almost at my place when I realize that I'm about to be dropped off and that will be it. I have a feeling that if nothing happens between Brett and I tonight when we're both a little tipsy and out of work mode, that nothing ever will. And the thought of never feeling his lips on mine, never feeling his hands on my body, is almost too much to bear.

I have to find a way to invite him up to my apartment without looking like I'm desperately trying to seduce him. I know Rita is staying at her boyfriend's place tonight. I can't help but think that if I can just get Brett alone up there, we will be unleashed and whatever is going to happen between us will happen. Maybe then I can get this desire out of my system and I can act a little more normally around him.

We're pulling onto my block when I turn to Brett to start and execute my plan to get him into my apartment. "So did you manage to get any other appointments set up tonight then?" I ask.

He nods his head, looking at me a little dazedly as though I have pulled him out of a deep thought. "Yes," he says. "I have several appointments set up for next week."

"Good," I reply.

The driver pulls up outside of my apartment building and I know this is my only shot. I can feel the blood rushing to my face and I am suddenly glad I'm beneath the cover of darkness so Brett can't see how uncomfortable I am.

"Maybe you should come up to my apartment and we'll have a quick drink and go over everything while the details are fresh in our minds. I'm a little worried that if we wait too long, we might forget something important. And Monday is a long way away."

Brett studies my face for a second, his expression giving nothing away.

I have no idea if he can read the intentions beneath the seemingly innocent invitation, and I have no idea whether he is going to say yes or no.

After what feels like forever, he gives a curt nod. "As you wish," he says, his tone cool and professional again. He turns his attention to the driver, leaning forward in his seat. "I'll call you when I'm ready to leave."

I can't help but wonder if he has really missed the message I'm sending him, or if he's just keeping his professional face on in front of the driver, but I'm suddenly awfully nervous. I'm nervous for what will happen if Brett understands my intentions, and I'm nervous for what will happen if he genuinely believes this is an important work discussion, because if that's the case, I really have nothing to tell him. I've already given him all of the information I have on the potential clients, and I am going to look so stupid when I have nothing else to tell him. How the hell will I explain that one? I guess I'll find out soon enough if he really believes this is about work.

9

Brett opens the door and starts to get out of the car.

I don't wait for him to come and open my door. I am too full of nervous energy to sit still and I get out of the car myself. I fish my keys out and open the front door.

Brett follows me in silence.

"Should we take the stairs? It's only one floor and the elevator takes forever to come. We could be up there before it even reaches us," I say, aware that I am babbling.

Brett gives me a half smile and nods. "Whatever you think."

I lead the way up the stairs and manage to get my apartment door unlocked. I push it open and flick on the lights, pleased that it's reasonably tidy. I gesture towards the living room area. "Make yourself comfortable," I say. "I'll get us a drink. I have wine or vodka."

"I think perhaps a coffee would be more appropriate," he says.

I nod, feeling my insides twisting and any hope of anything happening between us is dying now. I move into the kitchen and begin making us some coffee. I glance over my shoulder.

Brett hasn't sat down. He's standing in front of my bookshelf browsing the titles. His body language has changed completely and he looks closed off. The giddiness of the wine seems to have left him, and the slightly more relaxed, fun version of Brett has gone, replaced by the cold professional version.

As the coffee begins to brew, I turn and lean against the counter, watching Brett as he looks at my books. I'm trying my best to think of some feasible reason for luring him up here, but it's hard when so much of my attention is focused on his ass and how good it looks even through his jacket.

He turns and catches me watching him. He looks at me, a steely look in his eyes and no sign of the earlier teasing smile playing across his lips.

I hold his gaze, because what else can I do? I have come up with nothing I can say about any of the potential clients that he doesn't already know.

So I can either have him work out this was my awful attempt at seduction, or I can tell him something he already knows and make myself look ditzy. I don't even know which of those options is worse.

"You know, it's extremely unprofessional me being up here at such a late hour," Brett says.

His words sound like gentle teasing, maybe even flirting, but the steely expression hasn't left his eyes.

I don't think he's joking around anymore. "Why is it unprofessional? You're only here to talk about work."

The tiniest hint of a smile plays across his lips and then he eyeballs me with the same fierce intensity of a moment ago. "Oh. You're still playing that card," he says.

"Excuse me?" I say, sure I must have misheard him.

He shrugs and this time, his smile reaches his eyes. "Let's put it this way Opal. You finally have me here. If you want to talk about work, we can. But ask yourself this. Now, you have me where you want me, what do you really want to do to me?" He steps closer to me as he says it, crossing the living room. He stands a couple of feet away from me, staring at me with lust filled eyes.

My pussy is wet just looking at his eyes. I didn't mishear him and I didn't misunderstand him. He still wants this. He still wants me. All I have to do is tell him what I really want. But I can't find the words. His gaze throws me so completely that I just stand there staring at him. My chest is heaving with the fast, short breaths as I try to organise my thoughts.

Brett has an uncanny knack of switching lanes when I least expect it and leaving me staring after him, my mouth agape while I try to focus and keep up. It's both disconcerting and exhilarating at the same time.

I haven't decided yet whether I love it or hate it. I know if I don't say something soon, Brett is going to think I don't want him. I know how much I will regret it if I let him walk out of here after he's made it clear that if I want him, I can have him. This thought breaks the paralysis that has seized my body, and I push myself away from the counter, closing the gap between us even further.

"Well, what I really want to do to you is anything but professional," I say.

He smiles at me. The sexy smile where he only raises one half of his mouth. It's more of a smirk than a smile, but there's no malice in it, only lust.

I find it so damned sexy.

"That sounds ... interesting," he says.

"I think so." I'm still moving forward, and before I really know it, the gap between Brett and I is gone. I'm almost touching him, looking up into his dark and lust filled eyes. I stand up on my toes and reach up with my hands. I push my hands into Brett's hair like I've wanted to do for so long, and I pull his face down towards mine. He moves his head with no resistance, and I brush my lips over his, so lightly that I could believe we hadn't even touched if it wasn't for the way my lips tingle when I pull back slightly. I look him in the eye and then I move in for another go at his lips.

This time, our touch is anything but light.

Pressing my lips against Brett's lips, I moan slightly as I taste the sweetness of the wine on his lips. He moves his mouth in time with mine, but he makes no move to sweep me into his arms like I hoped he would. I don't let that put me off. Now we've started this, I don't think I could stop myself from touching Brett even if I wanted to which I most definitely don't.

I reach out, push his jacket off his shoulders and down his arms, letting it fall to the floor. I pull at his tie until it opens and I drop that down onto the floor too. I slowly open the buttons of his shirt, starting at the top one. I kiss down his neck and as I open each button, I move my mouth lower, running soft kisses over his chest and down his deliciously tight washboard stomach.

Brett makes no move to stop me, and when I glance up at him, he's watching me, his expression caught between amusement and lust. I run my tongue over his abs as I reach the last button. I know what will turn that look of amusement to total lust. I reach for the waistband of his trousers, ready to unleash his cock and get to my knees, but he stops me by reaching out and taking hold of the tops of my arms.

I look up questioningly and my breath sticks in my throat when I see the expression on his face. It's lust.

Pure, primal lust.

Pulling me back up, he presses his lips against mine, wrapping me in his arms.

His kiss is deeper, harder and more intense than mine was and I feel my whole body lighting up as he presses my body against him. My arms move around him, running up and down his back beneath his open shirt. I can feel the tight muscles there and I have an urge to dig my fingers into him, to really knead the muscles and make us one.

I can feel my breasts mashed against his chest and his hard cock pressed up against me. I move my hips, pressing myself against his cock and rubbing against it.

Groaning into my mouth, his hands go into my hair, pulling out my clip and setting all of my hair free. Brett's tongue pushes deeper into my mouth and I rub my own tongue across it, wanting to taste every part of his mouth. He moves his lips away from mine, kissing down my neck and pushing the strap of my dress to one side. He kisses along my shoulder blade as one of his hands snakes beneath my dress.

Brett's touch consumes me.

He pushes my panties to one side, his fingers slipping between my wet lips and finding my throbbing clit. I moan as he presses down on it, sending sparks of fire through my body and I sag against him slightly. He works me until I am on the verge of climaxing, my breath catching in my throat in quiet whimpers, and then he moves his fingers away from me, pulling my panties down. I step out of them and he moves his head back, looking deep into my eyes.

My clit is throbbing, my orgasm hovering on the brink of an explosion but not quite there yet. I know Brett knows exactly what he's doing to me. That he's leaving me desperate for more on purpose.

I don't have to wait long for more though. Brett picks me up and lifts my dress above my waist. He deposits me on the counter top. I spread my legs eagerly, hoping for his touch on my clit once more. He gets his trousers open then pushes them and his boxer shorts down. He steps between my spread legs and smiles at me, a smile that sends my temperature soaring.

Reaching around, I grab his ass. I can't wait any longer, so pulling him closer to me as I scoot forward on the counter. He smiles and puts his hands on my hips. He kisses my neck again as I close my eyes and throw my head back, moaning as goose bumps trail their way down my neck and over my chest.

One of Brett's hands leaves my hips and I feel him moving back from me slightly. I lift my head back up and open my eyes a tiny bit in time to see him positioning his cock at the edge of my pussy. He slams into me with no warning, and my eyes fly wide open as he fills me right up. I gasp as pleasure spreads through my pussy and up into my stomach.

Wrapping my legs around Brett's waist, I pull him into me deeper as he begins to thrust. I push my palms against his bare chest and kiss him deeply on the mouth as he strokes inside of me.

I move my hands around to his back, clutching him tightly against me. I lower my hands down to his ass, pushing him inside me even further, wanting him to fill every inch of me. I can hear myself panting and moaning as his cock brings my pussy to life.

He kisses my neck again, and I let my head fall back, my thoughts spinning out of control as desire floods me. I gasp as Brett ups the pace of his thrusts, slamming into me again and again. I can feel the orgasm that was hovering in the background rushing back, and this time, Brett doesn't leave me wanting for anything.

All of the pent up desire I have felt over the last two days, all of the dirty thoughts I have had about Brett, all come together in this moment and when my climax hits me, it hits me hard. My pussy clenches around Brett's cock, making him moan low in his throat, a noise so full of lust that it only pushes me further over the edge.

My whole body tingles, my skin heating up, my nerves buzzing with ecstasy. My clit is going wild, pulsing and throbbing as my pussy contracts again, so tightly that Brett is held in place for a second.

I gasp in a breath and let it out in a strangled scream that turns into Brett's name somewhere along the way and ends in a pained sounding moan as the pleasure consumes me completely.

Closing my eyes, I'm riding the waves that spread out through my whole body, each one reaching a little further than the one before it. I feel myself come, my pussy clenching once more and a rush of warm, wet liquid running from me.

Brett moans loudly as my juices flood him and he pushes his hands into my hair again, tugging it and making my scalp sting. He tugs my head into position and kisses me so roughly I feel like my lips are being skinned. But I don't care, because it feels so good to be this close to him, and to know that I am effecting him every bit as much as he's effecting me. My pussy twitches slightly as my orgasm begins to fade and my breath comes in gasping pants while I try to make up for the lack of oxygen as my orgasm squeezes my lungs to emptiness.

Brett pulls back from my kiss and with one last, hard thrust, his face contorts as he comes hard. He moans again, saying my name in that hot, husky voice.

I feel him spurting into me, his seed warm and welcome inside of me. His cock pulses, and another spurt of heat fills me. His whole body goes taut and he clings to me, holding me tightly against him.

His cock slips out of me, but he stays in place, standing between my legs and holding me in his arms. I wrap my heavy feeling arms around him and we both relax, trying to get our breathing back under control. I have dreamed of this moment since I first clapped eyes on Brett, but nothing could have prepared me for this. Even in my wildest fantasies, I didn't expect him to be that good. I have never orgasmed like that before.

I thought this would get Brett out of my system, make it easier to be around him without being distracted by what I wanted to do to him. I see now I was wrong about that. Having Brett, feeling him moving inside of me, has only made me want him more.

I almost protest when he finally pulls back from me.

He smiles down at me as he pulls his boxer shorts and pants back up. He kisses the top of my head.

"Wow," I manage.

"My thoughts exactly." He finishes buttoning his trousers and starts on his shirt.

I'm suddenly conscious of the fact I'm still sitting on the counter top, my pussy totally on show. I close my legs and hop down from the counter top.

Brett watches me as I retrieve my panties.

I pass him his tie and jacket from the ground.

"Is that a hint?" he says. "You've had what you want and now I should just go?"

"What? No!" I exclaim, horrified that he would think such a thing. I only handed him his clothes because I suddenly feel awkward again, very much aware that I have just seduced my boss.

"I'm joking Opal." Brett laughs.

"Oh," I manage. I say it again and laugh, relief flooding me.

"I probably should go though," he adds.

I nod, although everything in me is telling me not to let him go yet. To beg him to stay the night. To do that again, but slower, drawing it out, savouring every second of it. I don't say anything though. It would seem too humiliating to beg him to stay.

"That probably shouldn't have happened," Brett says.

There's no *probably* about it. It shouldn't have happened at all. If Mr. Connell finds out, I know I will be fired. I can't believe I've risked the career I've spent so long building for a couple of minutes of fun. But oh my God, was it worth it. And besides, it's not likely that Brett is going to call his father and tell him what just happened.

Releasing a grunting sound, I hope Brett takes it as an agreement. He's right, I can't quite bring myself to say the words out loud and risk cheapening what we have just done.

"For what it's worth, I'm glad it did though," he adds with a smile that is almost shy.

"Me too," I reply. That's definitely something I can agree with out loud in real words.

He smiles as he puts his jacket on then stuffs his tie into the pocket. He reaches out and brushes his fingers across my cheek and then he kisses me softly on the mouth. "I guess I'll see you on Monday then."

I nod, already dreading the moment when I have to face him again. His softness is gone from his voice now and he's all business again.

"I trust that I don't need to remind you that this must stay between us," he says.

"Of course," I say quickly.

"And that it can never happen again," he adds.

I nod, biting my lip to try and keep my disappointment from showing. *Just what did you expect Opal? You put it on a plate and he took it. It's not like he's going to want to keep doing this. And even if he does, you have to say no. You can't risk your career like this.* This happening once, I can tell myself I got caught up in the moment and let it happen. If it keeps happening, then I can't even pretend that to myself.

Brett turns away from me and heads for the door to my apartment. "I'll call my driver from downstairs," he says. "See you Monday." With that, he's gone.

I don't know whether to dance around my apartment in joy because of the way he made me feel as I came, or whether to curl into a ball and sob because it's over between us before it even really begun.

I'm really too shell shocked to do much of anything. I can't believe that really happened. I move as though in a trance and pour myself a cup of coffee from the pot I brewed earlier. I move to the couch and sit sipping the coffee, trying to make sense of a world where a man like Brett Connell could want me, even if only for a few minutes.

My phone beeps and I look around for my purse. I spot it and go to retrieve it, hoping for a crazy moment that it's Brett. It's not. It's Gary, professing his love for me. Angrily, I close my text messages. There are several missed calls from an unknown number, and I know that's Gary too. With a sigh, I switch the phone off and go back to sipping my coffee.

Eventually, my eyelids start to feel heavy, so I switch off the lights and go through to my bedroom. I lay down in my dress, unable to find the energy to bother getting changed or taking my makeup off. I lay in a cloud of post orgasmic joy and relive what Brett and I have just done. I finally fall asleep with a wide grin on my face.

10

Monday morning comes around a lot quicker than I would have liked it to. Instead of being excited at the thought of seeing Brett again, I just feel nervous. My stomach swirls sickly like it has all weekend.

I spent all of Saturday and Sunday trying to make sense of what happened, and I still haven't been able to decide how to handle the moment I see Brett again. I want to be professional about it all, but I don't want him to think I'm cold, or that I'm the sort of girl who hops into bed with a guy and then just writes him off. But at the same time, we both know nothing else can happen, and I'm worried if I act overly familiar with him, he might think I am trying to get it to happen again between us.

I'm just glad Rita ended up spending the whole weekend at her boyfriend's place and I didn't have to fend off a barrage of questions from her. She would have taken one look at me and known something was off and I would have ended up telling her everything. I don't even know how I feel about any of this yet, so I am far from ready to start trying to analyze it with someone else. Particularly, someone like Rita who can read me so well. She knows me almost better than I know myself and she might just pull put some answers that I'm just not ready for yet.

Showering quickly, I then get dressed. I don't allow myself to agonize over my outfit. I put on a sensible navy blue shift dress, the kind I always wear for work, and navy court shoes. I don't need a jacket as it's warm enough outside. I allow myself to put a thin black belt around my waist and at least give myself some shape, but that's it. My makeup is sensible, natural looking, and I pin my hair up in a messy bun, just like I would any day for work.

Gazing at myself in the mirror, I decide I'll do. I look like I'm going to work and that's all I am doing. The fact that Brett will also be there is neither here nor there. It's one thing letting my hair down at a party, but I'm not going to let any of this effect my work in any way.

Even as I tell myself this, I know it's not true. My stomach is rolling and my heart is beating so fast, it feels like palpitations. My palms are sweaty and I can feel a sheen of sweat coating my back too. I take a deep breath as a wave of dizziness seizes me. I reach out and flatten my palm against the wall to steady myself. Nausea rolls over me in waves and I take long, slow breaths, trying to get it to pass. Dots of white light dance in front of my vision and my stomach cramps as another wave of nausea rolls over me.

I know deep breaths aren't going to get rid of it as my stomach cramps again. Saliva floods my mouth and my throat starts to tighten. I push myself away from the wall and run blindly for the bathroom. I throw myself down onto my knees in front of the toilet just in time as my breakfast comes up.

Leaning back, I try to compose myself, but another cramp hits and I find myself hanging over the toilet, retching and retching, even when there's nothing left to come up. I try to tell myself its food poisoning, but I know better. I've worked myself up into such a state while thinking about facing Brett that I've actually made myself physically sick.

I stay on the ground for another couple of minutes, but the nausea seems to have faded. I still feel a little lightheaded and I sway slightly on my feet as I move to the sink. I swill my mouth out and brush my teeth again. I look at myself in the mirror. I look pale and sweaty and my head is still spinning. There is no way I'm going in to work to face Brett looking like this.

That makes me feel slightly better, as I leave the bathroom and go back to my bedroom in search of my phone, I even start to feel hungry. It makes sense. I have just lost my break-fast and I didn't eat much yesterday, so the nerves were already starting to kick in then.

I call the office and speak to one of the receptionists. She asks if I want to be put through to Brett,

"No," I say, a little too quickly. "I mean no thank you. He's a busy man and he won't need me bothering him. Please just let him know I won't be in today."

"Ok, feel better soon," she replies.

"Thanks." I end the call and sit down on my bed, wondering what to do with my day. Now I know I don't have to face Brett today, I feel better, but I can't risk being caught out and about. I shrug my shoulders. A pyjama and movie day it is then.

My phone rings and I pick it up. My stomach cramps again when I see the number. It's Mr. Connell's personal office line. That means it's Brett. I debate ignoring the call, but I know I can't do that and expect to keep my job. I press answer and bring the phone up to my ear tentatively like it's a bomb about to explode at any minute. "H-hello," I stutter.

"Opal, it's Brett." His voice sounds formal, even kind of angry. He's not calling to see if I'm ok, that's for sure.

"Hi," I say.

"I'm not sure what's going on, but I just got a message from one of the secretaries saying you won't be in today. I'm sure that's a misunderstanding right?" he says.

"Actually no, it's not. I think I've got a touch of food poisoning and I won't be in today."

"That's not an option Opal. No offense, but my father had a heart attack and he was still working from his hospital bed. I'm sure you can come in feeling a little bit sickly."

I want to tell him it's more than that, but I don't want him picturing me with my head down the toilet, throwing my guts up. I really don't want to go in though. If I thought facing him before would have been hard, this incident has only made it ten times worse. I never should have allowed myself to bail in the first place. "I—ummm."

"Opal, this isn't open to discussion," Brett says, cutting me off. "We have a busy day today with a couple of important meetings and I need you in. I'll expect to see you in this office within the hour."

He hangs up leaving me staring at the phone open mouthed. I am so angry. How dare he just dismiss my illness like that and demand I come in. And then to not even wait for an answer. I was wrong about Brett. He might be drop dead gorgeous, but he's not a nice man. It doesn't matter that my illness isn't exactly real. He doesn't know that.

I sit on the spot, fuming for a moment. I could just not go in and when he reports me to HR, I can explain I was ill and then tell them what happened. Mr. Connell would take my side when he hears what happened, I'm almost certain of it.

Thinking of Mr. Connell sends a rush of guilt through me. He trusted me to help Brett run his company in his time of need, and I am letting him down greatly. I got drunk, seduced my boss and then called in sick because I freaked out at the thought of seeing him again, so soon after it. And I know if I did have a touch of food poisoning as I had claimed to have, that if Mr. Connell had called me and told me he needed me in anyway, I would have gone in without any hesitation. Of course, he wouldn't have been such a dick about it, but still, I would have done it with no complaints.

I need to put my personal feelings about Brett to one side and just treat him like my boss. And that means going in to work, even when I don't feel one hundred percent. Perhaps it means that even more so than ever now, considering my illness is only a result of my nerves at my own stupid actions catching up with me.

With a sigh, I stand and grab my purse and keys. I dash back into my bedroom and fix my lipstick and then I head out. I head to the office telling myself to let the anger go. I am showing up. I'm showing Brett I am a professional and can still be relied on. I just have to get through today and then everything will be fine.

I reach the office quickly and go straight up to my office. Brett said he expected me in within the hour and I am here within half of that time. Surely, that shows dedication. I still feel kind of angry and although I'm trying to contain it, in one sense, it's a good thing, because the anger has gotten rid of my nerves and at least, I don't feel sick anymore.

I boot up my computer and begin responding to emails. I have been working for about ten minutes when my desk phone rings. The light is on to show me the call is coming from Mr. Connell's office, and the nerves come back with a vengeance. I swallow hard and pick up the phone. "Hello."

"Ah Opal, you're here. Good," Brett says briskly. "Can you come to my office please? Now."

"Right away." I hang up the phone and stand up on slightly shaky legs. Please let it just be a query about a client account I think to myself as I make my way to Brett's office. I tap on the door and Brett shouts for me to come in. I take a deep breath and push the door open.

Brett is sitting in his father's chair looking at the computer on the desk in front of him. He glances up at me as I step in.

I feel my heart sink. He is as cold and distant as he's ever been, but beneath that cool professional exterior, I can see he's pissed off with me. Great. He looks like a totally different person to the guy I had sex with in my kitchen on Friday night. A different person to the one who laughed with me at the party before we went back to my apartment and ruined everything. He even looks more distant than he did before the party, and I really didn't think that was possible.

This is all I need.

"Sit down please," Brett says.

I stand just inside of the door fidgeting my fingers together in front of me. I move towards his desk and take a seat, keeping my hands away from each other. Whatever this is, I don't want to look nervous. It will make it look like I have something to hide and I haven't. "What can I do for you?" I ask brightly, hoping his anger isn't at me and we can just get down to business.

"You can start by telling me why you thought it was appropriate to call in sick today," he says, dismissing any notion of this just being pushed under the rug. "I really thought better of you after my father's recommendation of you, and I didn't expect you to be the type of person who pretends to be ill to get out of work."

If only it was as simple as me wanting to get out of work. That I could have easily ignored and came in anyway. "That's quite some accusation," I say. "And for the record, it's a baseless accusation. I wasn't lying. I have come in because you said you needed me. I still feel under the weather and I would appreciate it if we could get to the point, because clearly there's something important you want to discuss with me to ask me to come in when I'm not feeling very well." My voice comes out steady, my tone cool and professional and I surprise myself. I was half expecting my voice to break and give away how utterly nervous I am.

Brett raises an eyebrow at my little lecture, but he doesn't lose his composure for even a second. "I asked you to come in because it's your job to be here Opal. I am a little disappointed that you're being so immature about this. Yes, we fucked a couple of nights ago, but that shouldn't be affecting your work."

I just stare at him, my jaw hanging open. I can't believe he just said that. I don't know whether to be angry, sad or amused by his bluntness. My body decides for me and a little laugh squeezes out of my throat. I try to cover it with a cough, but I'm too late.

Brett glares at me. "Is something funny?"

"Just your assumption that me being ill is anything to do with what happened between us."

He waves away my words and shakes his head. "It clearly has everything to do with it Opal. If you think I can't see that, then you're either deluding yourself, or you're hugely underestimating me. What happened between us was a mistake. I should never have allowed myself to get caught up in the moment like that, and for that I apologize. It won't ever happen again."

I open my mouth to respond, but Brett just keeps on talking like I'm not really there, "Now that's out of the way, let's move on shall we? I do have a business matter to discuss with you. I have a meeting with Brice Newcomb later on today. I know you said his company is in the IT sector, but can you elaborate on that? I'd like to know the ins and outs of his business before I put together a package for him."

I'm still reeling at how this worked out. First Brett scolded me like I was some silly school girl and now, he's back to work talk like it's normal to talk to an employee that way? I can't believe how easily he just brought up what happened between us, and then just dismissed it equally as easily. I mean what the actual fuck is that all about?

I manage to hold my emotions in check though and I give him the run down on Brice Newcomb's business, including the bits I know he won't find on any official documentation.

"Thank you." Brett nods when I'm finished talking. He has been taking notes.

At least I know he's serious about the business. My anger has mostly fizzled out now and I just want to get through today and then have things go back to the way they were between us before any of this happened.

Brett peers at me as though he's studying my face, looking for something there.

"What?" I ask, reaching up to touch my mouth, self conscious that I have something on my face or something.

"Nothing," he says. "I was just thinking you do look a little pale, and if you need to go home, then just go."

Somehow, that is the final insult and I feel my temper flaring up again. If that is his idea of an apology for accusing me of lying to get out of work and acting unprofessionally, then he's in for a shock, because it doesn't even come close to making me want to forgive him. "It's fine," I snap. "I'm sure I can make it to the toilet in time if I need to. Is there anything else you need?"

Brett shakes his head, watching me with amusement again.

11

God, he's so fucking arrogant. I can't believe I ever found him attractive. He's just a massive douche bag. I get up and leave the office without another word, no longer caring anymore if he knows I'm annoyed at him. I kind of want him to know. It's not okay to treat people like this. I don't know what he's used to at his own company. Mr. Connell might be formal, but at least he always treats his employees with respect.

I sit at my desk, anger running through my veins as I go back to my emails. It's going to be a long day if I can't let go of this anger, but try as I might, I just can't do it. It takes me a while, but I realize that for all Brett has been so high and mighty about the whole thing and pissed me off, it's not really him I'm annoyed at. It's myself. Because everything he said was true.

I did call in sick and although I was actually sick, it wasn't like I was ill, it was just nerves and I knew it. I called in sick because I didn't want to face Brett after what happened on

Friday, just like he said I had. I hate that he sees through me so easily.

Somehow, I get through the rest of the day. I'm polite, pleasant and friendly to Brett when he comes in, and whenever any other staff members are around, but when we are alone, I don't speak to him. I barely even look at him. I know he notices, but he doesn't care enough to ask me about it, and that suits me just fine.

I don't want to give Brett any other reason to be annoyed with me, so when five o'clock rolls around and I should be finishing for the day, I stay and finish up the report I am working on. At 6:15 when it's finished, I print it off and go to Brett's office. I tap on the door and wait.

"Come in," he calls.

I go in.

He looks shocked to see me. "I thought you'd left."

I hold the report up for him to see and then put it on his desk. "I wanted to get this finished first."

He opens his mouth as though he's going to say something, but then he closes it again and just nods. "Thanks."

Turning, I head out of the office.

"Hold on a second and I'll walk down with you," Brett says.

I can't think of any good reason to say no. I already have my purse with me and Brett can see I'm clearly ready to leave. I wait mutely as he closes down his computer and grabs his jacket and briefcase.

Oh God, maybe he has a date, I think to myself with horror. Don't even go there, I tell myself.

I think about asking him how come he's leaving so soon, but he'd be perfectly within his rights to tell me to mind my own damned business. I don't want to give him the satisfaction of being able to do that. We walk to the elevator in silence.

Brett leans forward and presses the button and we wait.

I twirl a loose tendril of hair around my finger as we wait. I can feel myself getting nervous again. Why would he have asked me to wait for him if he didn't have something to say to me? My stomach rolls and I will it to be still.

Please don't throw up here, I think to myself, although if I did, maybe then Brett would feel like an asshole for dragging me in to work today.

Finally, the elevator car arrives. I get a sinking feeling when I see it's empty. Great. More awkward silence. Why didn't he just let me go and give me a couple of minutes to get out of sight before he left?

I press the button for the ground floor and the elevator begins to move.

"I'm sorry I was so harsh to you this morning," Brett says quietly once we're moving.

Shrugging my shoulders, I lie, "I'm over it."

"Well, I'm not. I handled it horribly and I'm sorry. I guess I was just ashamed of myself. I don't generally fraternise with employees like that, and I'm sorry for that too," he adds.

I soften ever so slightly. "Believe it or not, I don't make a habit of sleeping with people I work with either. Why don't we just forget about it?"

"Yes," Brett agrees. "My thoughts exactly. Which is why I think a temporary transfer for you would be a good idea. I'm only going to be here until my father is well enough to return, so it'll only be for a few months. You can choose your department and I'll make sure you're well rewarded financially for the inconvenience."

Anger surges through me once more. He thinks he can have his fun with me and then palm me off to another department once I become a problem to him? *Well, fuck that. The offer of a financial reward too? I mean that doesn't make me feel like a whore at all.*

I open my mouth to tell Brett exactly what I think of his bright idea when the elevator stops and the doors ping open.

Brett doesn't even look at me.

"Think about it," he says as he steps out and hurries away from me.

At least now, I know why he wanted to walk out of the building with me. He would never have said that in his office, knowing I would likely yell loud enough for half of the building to hear me. Well, if he thinks I won't do that in the lobby, then maybe he's the one who has hugely underestimated me.

I step out and rush across the lobby to catch up with Brett. I am almost half way across the lobby when my phone rings. Dammit. I snatch it out of my bag and answer it without looking at the screen. I'm expecting it to be Rita, calling to ask me to pick up dinner, and I plan on telling her I'll call her back.

It isn't Rita's voice that greets me, it's Gary's, "I see you've switched your phone back on at last." He sounds triumphant, like he's won some sort of prize.

I sigh. I really don't need this right now. "Gary when someone changes their phone number and doesn't give you their new one, there's usually a reason for that," I say.

"Yes, I know," he agrees. "And I know why you did it. You wanted me to prove my love for you by finding it for myself."

"What? No. Not even close. Gary this is crazy. Just ... just stop calling me and stay out of my life," I snap.

"I just wanted to ask you something real quick," Gary says, ignoring my anger.

"What?" I figure it might be quicker just to answer him than it will be to ignore him and have him keep bothering me. I'm still making my way across the lobby as I talk and I turn right as I leave the building, heading for the car park. I might still be able to catch up with Brett yet.

"Who were you with on Friday night when I called you? And don't lie to me Opal. I could hear a man's voice," Gary says.

"It's none of your damned business," I snap. I should have just hung up. I should have known his question would be something ridiculous.

"Of course, it's my business. You're my girl Opal and I don't like the idea of you with other men and making a fool of me. I'm willing to let it go this once, but just keep in mind that we haven't broken up. We're only on a break."

"Oh my God Gary, listen to yourself. We're not a break. It's been weeks. We have broken up."

"No we haven't," he insists.

He's crazy and I know I can't reason with crazy. "Just stay out of my life," I say, ending the call and dropping my phone back into my purse.

It starts ringing again almost immediately, but I ignore it. I have reached the car park and I look around quickly, trying to spot Brett. I can't see him anywhere. A silver car drives past me heading out of the car park and into the street and I curse when I see that Brett is driving the car.

Thanks Gary, thanks a fucking bunch.

*A*lmost before I've even sat down at my desk the next day, I am summoned to Brett's office. I already know what it's going to be about, and I have already decided how I am going to handle it. I'm not letting him push me around and transfer me somewhere.

It's all right him saying it's temporary, but how will I explain it to Mr. Connell? I'm sure Brett would come up with some explanation for it that doesn't make me look too bad, but whatever he says, Mr. Connell is going to think that either I'm not as good at my job as he thought I was, or that I don't play nicely with others, and neither of those options bode well for me at the company.

Plus, I don't see why I should be the one made to move. I wasn't the only one fucking on the kitchen counter. Why should I be punished for something Brett and I both did?

I have also decided that I'm not going to give him a piece of my mind after all. I won't give him the satisfaction of thinking he has that kind of power over me. Screw that. I get up and go to Brett's office, only entering once he calls for me to come in. He smiles at me coolly and tells me to sit down, which I do.

"I just wondered if you've given any thought to my suggestion of a temporary transfer," Brett says.

Crap, he's still so damned hot. I try to avoid looking at his eyes, and I end up looking at his mouth instead, but all I can think of when I see his mouth is what his lips felt like on mine, and I think maybe looking at his mouth is even worse than looking into his eyes.

Clearing my throat, I smile politely. "I have thought about it and I've decided to decline the offer."

Brett raises an eyebrow. He clearly wasn't expecting that one.

I resist the urge to grin.

"I must admit I'm a little bit surprised," he says.

"Why?" I dare to ask.

"Well you seemed so ... so thrown yesterday. I thought you want to avoid feeling like that every day until my father returns."

"Look Brett, let's cut the bullshit ok?" I say.

He looks taken aback but he doesn't interrupt.

I go on, "I was pissed off yesterday because you accused me of faking an illness to get out of work, something I've never done and have no intention of starting doing now. It had nothing to do with what happened between us. I know you think you're the hot shit and you have some sort of effect on me, but honestly, you don't. We got tipsy and did something stupid. So unless you're regularly going to call me a liar and doubt my integrity, I really see no reason for me to transfer departments."

He looks ready to argue.

Now, I play the final ace I have up my sleeve, because I really want to stay here. I love my job, and more than that, I want to prove to Brett that he has no effect on me. That I am a true professional. "Unless of course I'm having some sort of effect on you. I mean I'd hate to think I was distracting you from your work," I say with a smile.

"Not at all," Brett says through gritted teeth. "If that's your decision then that's fine. That will be all for now."

I stand and smile sweetly at him. Although inside, I'm doing a victory dance as I reach the door.

Brett calls after me, "Opal?"

I glance back.

"Well played," he says.

For a second, I see a flash of the smile he wore on Friday night and I feel a shiver go down my spine. I flash him a quick smile back and leave the office before he can see the effect he's having on me. I might have won this battle, but I know it won't be the only one I'll face, and I'm damned if I'm going to show anything but cool courtesy to Brett now.

12

The rest of the week passes swiftly, with virtually no hiccups. Brett managed to secure two of the three potential clients from the party and he also brought in a couple of new prospects that he had been talking to of his own accord, so we were both damned busy all week, which I think helped.

I have spent the week acting like the perfect personal assistant and not letting Brett get under my skin for even a second. More than once, I caught him watching me when he thought I wasn't looking, and I just have to hope he didn't catch me doing the exact same thing.

By the time I reached my desk this morning, I almost convinced myself I was over Brett, that I no longer even found him attractive. It is a lie of course, but I thought maybe if I tell myself enough, I will start to believe it.

It's funny to think that this time last week, I was a tongue tied wreck around Brett. I guess a week can make a big difference.

I glance at my watch. It's half past one and I know I need to leave the office now if I'm to make it to Mr. Connell's place at two. He called this morning, saying it had been just over a week since Brett took over running the business and he would like to have a meeting with the both of us to see how everything was going. I tried to talk him out of it, but he wouldn't hear of it. So he eventually convinced me by reminding me it was Friday and I would get an early finish this way as I could go home after the meeting. The meeting is being held at Mr. Connell's home as he's out of the hospital now.

Pick up the pile of files I have already gathered together and copied, I know Mr. Connell will want them left at his place so he can familiarize himself with the new accounts. I've also made myself a couple of pages of notes in case Mr. Connell has any questions about the new clients. I stuff those into my purse and sling it over my shoulder.

Brett has already left, telling me he had a lunch appointment and would meet me there. I pointed out there was nothing in his diary about a lunch appointment and he told me the appointment was to have lunch with his mom. It means he'd already be at the house when I arrive, giving me another reason to make damned sure I'm not late for this.

I wonder fleetingly if they'll have already discussed the important points before I get there, but I dismiss the idea. Neither of the men would think twice about just telling me I wasn't needed and risking hurting my feelings. If Mr. Connell wants me there, it's for a reason.

I call a cab as I go down in the elevator. I go to the street to wait for a taxi and it's there within five minutes. I give the driver Mr. Connell's address and sit back in the seat to look out of the window. I'm not nervous about this meeting. I know our existing clients and the new accounts inside and out. So there's nothing Mr. Connell can ask me that I won't be able to answer. And I have my notes just in case my mind goes blank or anything.

I pay for the cab when we pull up outside of Mr. Connell's large house and get out. I ring the door bell and wait.

Mrs. Connell answers the door, dressed in turquoise leggings and a white flowy tunic style blouse.

I wait for the glaring and the lectures.

Instead, she smiles at me as she pulls the door open further. "Come on in Opal."

I step inside.

Mrs. Connell closes the front door and turns to me, looking suddenly awkward. "I wanted to apologize to you Opal. I was rude to you at the hospital and I'm sorry," she says.

"Don't worry, it's fine." I smile. "I know you were worried about Mr. Connell."

"I swear that man will be the death of me." She nods, looking relieved that I've accepted her apology without making a big deal out of it. She points down the hallway. "They're in my husband's study. Third door on the right."

"Thank you." I follow her directions and knock on the closed door.

"Yes," Mr. Connell barks.

I push the door open and poke my head around it.

Mr. Connell smiles when he sees me. "Come in, come in, Don't be shy Opal."

I step all of the way into the room and close the door quietly.

Mr. Connell is still smiling at me, but it's a strained smile and Brett doesn't even look up at me. He sits looking out of the window, his face a mask of anger.

Instantly, I can feel the tension between the two of them and I half wish I would have invited myself along for the lunch to save this from happening.

I approach the recliner where Mr. Connell sits.

Brett sits beside him in a normal armchair and there's another one there for me.

Mr. Connell waves towards the seat.

A horrible thought occurs to me then as I take my seat. What if the tension in the room is because Brett has told his father about what we did and told him he can't work with me anymore? Am I about to be fired? I dismiss the thought as quickly as it came, reminding myself once more that Brett isn't going to discuss his sex life with his father. He might have told him there's a bit of tension between us, but if that's the case, then that's not exactly grounds for me to be fired.

"How are you dear?" Mr. Connell asks me.

"I'm fine thank you. How are you feeling?" I reply.

"A lot better thank you," Mr. Connell says. He lowers his voice and grins conspiratorially at me. "I just need to convince Yvonne I'm not about to drop dead and then everything can go back to normal."

I laugh quietly and shake my head. I feel relieved that he's joking around with me. Whatever has happened between Mr. Connell and Brett to cause this awful atmosphere has nothing to do with me.

"Right, let's get down to business then. Brett informs me we have several new clients. Why don't we start by you filling me in on them, Opal?"

I nod, happy to be getting down to business. I start to tell Mr. Connell about the new clients – who they are, what their businesses entail, what we're doing for them, and perhaps most importantly, how it affects our bottom line. The whole time I'm talking, I can feel Brett's eyes on me. I try to ignore his gaze, but it's hard and a couple of times, I stutter a little as I talk.

Mr. Connell doesn't comment on my stuttering.

The more I glance up and catch Brett's eyes on me, the more conscious I am of the feel of him looking at me when I'm not looking back at him. It makes me feel good. There is no animosity in his look and it makes me think that maybe, just maybe, I am having an effect on him after all. This thought takes me to a dangerous place. A place where I allow myself to believe we can get past our blip and go back to how things were this time last week. Well, more accurately, how things were this time last week plus a couple of hours when we were at the dinner party and beyond it.

"Right, I think that about sums everything up," I say, a half hour later when I've briefed Mr. Connell on everything and gotten a glass of lemonade provided by Mrs. Connell. I glance over at Brett. "Unless you have anything to add?"

"No," he says coldly.

"Ok, what's going on here?" Mr. Connell says, looking at Brett and then at me. "You're being rude to Opal, Brett, and you Opal, can barely string a sentence together without stuttering and spluttering. What's happened between you two?"

"N-nothing," I say quickly, feeling my face warm. How the hell has he jumped to the conclusion that something has happened between us, just from this? The atmosphere in the room was bad before I even stepped into it, and if anything, it's thawed slightly since I came in. How can he blame this on me?

"I'm not convinced. Have you two been fighting about something?" Mr. Connell says. "Brett? Opal? Someone tell me what I'm missing here."

Brett smirks.

I blush again. Of course Mr. Connell didn't mean something like sex happened between us. He thinks we hate each other. He thinks Brett is looking at me so intensely because he hates me, and that I'm stuttering and spluttering because I'm very much aware of that. And Brett is smirking because the blush on my cheeks gave away exactly where my mind went.

"Honestly Mr. Connell, everything's great between us," I reassure him. "Right, Brett?"

"Right," Brett agrees.

"Hmm," Mr. Connell says. "Why don't I believe that? Anyway, it's not something I'm going to press you on, but I will say this. Whatever you two think of each other, it had better not affect any clients."

I just nod.

"Thank you for coming Opal. You've been very helpful. Please leave the files there, so I can go through them later. That will be all."

Standing, I leave the files in a neat pile on a small coffee table. "Thanks Mr. Connell. I hope you're feeling a lot better soon."

Brett stand as I start to leave.

"Actually Brett, there's something else I want to talk to you about," Mr. Connell says.

Brett sighs and sits back down.

I am out of the study and free of the terrible atmosphere. I breathe a sigh of relief as I make my way back along the hallway and outside. It's a nice day and I debate getting the bus back into town and then walking home, but I have no idea what time the buses run here, or even where I would catch one. I don't want to go back in and disturb Mrs. Connell. I will have to get a cab.

Opening my purse, I start digging around for my phone, pushing aside the pages and pages of hand written notes. I have finally gotten my hand on my phone when I hear a car engine. I look up as a black Mercedes pulls up at the curb and the window goes down.

"Are you calling a cab?" Brett asks, nodding towards the phone in my hand.

I nod.

"Don't bother. Get in and we'll take you home," he says.

I open my mouth to tell him no thank you, but movement catches my eye. I turn to look and see Mrs. Connell watching us out of the window. I really don't want her to mention to

Mr. Connell that I refused a lift from her son. Instead, I smile and nod. "Thanks." I walk around to the other side of the car as Brett's window slides back up. I get in and Brett gives his driver my address.

We pull away and Brett starts to speak, "You'll never guess what my father wanted me to hang back for."

He's right, I wouldn't and I am curious, especially when Brett was only in there a couple of minutes after I left. "What?"

"He reminded me of how valuable you are to the company and told me off for pissing you off."

I can't help but smile at the thought of Mr. Connell telling Brett I'm valuable to him. "Why were you so angry at me in there?" I ask.

"I wasn't angry at you. I was angry at him. I realize you probably thought I was staring daggers at you, but I was looking at you to stop myself from looking at him, because I knew if I looked at him for too long, I would have ended up snapping at him."

"Fair enough," I say, knowing better than to even ask what's going on between the two of them. Something is definitely going on though. Brett isn't exactly Mr. Chatty at the best of times, but he barely said a word through the whole meeting and now, he's talking to me like we're friends again. I can't work him out.

"Look Opal, do you think maybe we could call a truce? We got off on the wrong foot, and I know that was mostly my fault, but"

"Mostly your fault?" I interrupt him, raising my eyebrow at him.

"Ok, completely my fault." He smiles.

It's the smile that almost makes him look shy. The one that makes me melt inside and I feel myself returning the smile. "What the hell? Why not. Let's just start over with a clean slate,"

"Thanks." He turns to look out of the window, falling silent again.

I notice his hands in his lap. They're clenched into fists so tightly that his knuckles are white. I try to ignore it, but I can't and I eventually, work up the courage to ask him what's wrong. I don't really expect him to tell me, but I'll feel awful if I don't even try to get him to open a little and talk about whatever is bothering him. "Brett?" I say quietly.

He turns to look at me.

I plough ahead before I can change my mind, "What's wrong? I can see something is bothering you, so don't say it's nothing."

He looks at me for a couple of seconds as though he's deciding whether or not to tell me. He smiles as we turn a corner and pull onto my block. "I guess it's late for me to tell you now," he says.

Suddenly, I realize he wasn't thinking about whether or not to trust me, he is stalling. "Not necessarily. We could—shit!" I shout the last part, throwing myself off the seat and ducking down out of sight when I spot Gary sitting on the steps at the front of my apartment building. *Oh God, not now!*

13

"Opal? What is it?" Brett asks, looking down at me.

The car is slowing down and I ignore Brett for a moment, talking instead to the driver, "Please keep going. Just drop me off on the next block instead."

The driver looks into the rear view mirror at Brett.

He nods his head then looks back down at me as I remain crouched in the space between the front and the back seats. "What's going on?" he asks again. "Who is that man on your building's steps?"

I debate lying to him, but what would be the point? And besides, what could I tell him to explain my strange behaviour except the truth? That he's my landlord and I owe him rent money? I don't think so. I sigh, resigning myself to just telling Brett who Gary really is, "He's my ex boyfriend. Although, he seems to think there's still a chance for us. He's clingy and irritating, and to be honest, I would rather just wait around until he gets bored and goes away." It's not a lie exactly, although I have downplayed Gary's character some-what. To say he's clingy is an understatement, and although I would never admit it to Brett, I'm kind of worried that he won't get bored and go away. That he'll stay there until I eventually come home.

"Is he dangerous?" Brett asks me with a frown.

The car turns onto the next block and pulls into the curb.

Bouncing back up from the floorboard, I perch on the seat for a moment as my thighs scream at me. I shake my head. "No, he's harmless, just irritating." I hope that's true. I slide my body towards the door. "Thank you for the lift."

Brett touches my arm.

I breathe in audibly and look back at him.

His eyes search my face. "I don't like the idea of you wandering the streets waiting for him to go away. Would you like to hang out for a couple of hours instead?"

The stubborn part of me wants to say no, but luckily, that's not the part that's in charge of this choice. The part making the decisions right now is the part that really doesn't want to face Gary. I tell myself it's nothing to do with the tingling in my arm at Brett's touch. "That would be great," I say grate-fully. "Unless you have plans of course. I don't want to spoil your evening or anything."

"Well, now that you mention it, hanging out with someone I can laugh with would kind of spoil my plans to sit alone in front of the TV." Brett smirks.

I elbow him and laugh, but I settle back into the seat and that gives him his answer.

He leans forward slightly and talks to the driver, giving him an address I don't recognize. I don't ask where we're going. I don't care. Anywhere with Brett will be better than being stuck here, forced to face Gary or risking having to wander the streets all night.

We drive in comfortable silence for a time. I look out of the window, trying to get my bearings, but we're driving though a part of the city I don't know very well. We turn onto a road that seems to lead out into the countryside. We drive down a narrow road lined by bushes and the driver pulls over.

Brett starts to get out of the car.

"Wait," I say. "Where are we?"

"What's wrong?" Brett smirks. "Scared you'll get dirty or something?" He gets out of the car without waiting for an answer.

I roll my eyes as I clamber out of my side and look around. We're really in the middle of nowhere, but I'm not particularly afraid of getting dirty, but if Brett wants to go walking through the fields, then I'm certainly not going to be the one to try and stop him.

"This way," Brett says, walking alongside the bushes.

Shrugging, I run a few steps to catch up with him and fall into step beside him. "So, do you come here often?" I joke.

"Oh, I'm a regular hiker," Brett jokes back.

I shake my head. He's clearly not going to tell me why we're out here, and I'm not going to give him the satisfaction of keeping asking him. Right now, I'm just pleased we seem to have slipped back into a bit more of a friendly relationship.

Brett pauses and looks both ways along the road, so I think we're about to cross the road, but instead, he takes hold of my hand and pulls me towards the bushes. "Through here." He squeezes through a tiny gap in the bushes and pulls me through behind him before I can protest or ask him any questions.

"What the ..." I start as I stumble out of the bushes. I trail off when I see where we are. A golf course is spread out before us, the green expanse of neat lawn and sand bunkers seeming to go on forever.

"Not too shabby, right?" Brett is still holding my hand in his and he starts to walk onto the course pulling me along behind him. "I hope you don't mind sand," he winks at me, looking back over his shoulder.

The wink and the feel of my hand in his leaves me speechless and I just shake my head. In that moment, I would have followed him into a field freshly spread with manure. Sand is nothing.

He leads me to one of the larger bunkers and we slip and slide down the edge and into the center where it's flatter. He sits down and pulls me down beside him.

"Are we allowed to be out here?" I ask, looking around nervously, waiting for a security guard to appear over the edge of the bunker and chase us away.

"Sure we are," Brett replies.

I'm not entirely convinced that's true. "So why did we sneak in through a gap in the bushes?" I challenge him.

Brett grins and lays back, folding his hands beneath his head and looking up at the sky. "Relax Opal," he smiles as I peer down at him. "I own the club. I sneaked us in the back way because I couldn't be bothered with making nice with everyone on the way through the club that's all."

I peer at him for a moment longer, waiting for him to laugh or something, but he doesn't. Something tells me he's telling the truth. I decide to believe him. I lay back beside him on the sand. It's warm on my back and I have to admit it feels nice lying here. I can almost imagine we're at the beach somewhere. It's just a shame I'm in a work's dress rather than a swim suit.

"Remember I told Mr. Simmons at the party that I'd been in France for a year expanding my business?" Brett says.

"Mmhmm," I say.

"My father tried to block the deal, but he failed. I was opening another club in the South of France. This one was my first one and it will always be my baby, but the real money is where the rich tourists are," he says.

His revelation surprises me a little and I push myself up onto my elbows, "I thought your business was asset management, the same as your father's?"

"Oh, fuck no," Brett says with a visible shudder. "My parents wanted me to take over the company, and as such, they primed me all of my life with the knowledge of how the business works. That's how I was able to step in for my father. But it's never been anything I would choose to get involved with. There's plenty of ways to make money, and I'd rather make mine by giving people something they can enjoy, rather than investing money and managing assets."

"I know what you mean," I say, laying back down beside him. "But for me, I kind of enjoy the assets side of things. You know, the thrill of the chase, finding a perfect investment opportunity for a client and then playing the game until they get it."

"You like the thrill of the chase huh?" Brett says a smile in his voice. "And then playing the game?"

"Yeah, I always though asset management sounded pretty boring, but when I first started working for your father, it was a case of a job is a job. But then I started to see how the business worked and I guess I was hooked."

"It sounds more like a plan to catch a guy. Chase them, play them, and toss them away," Brett says.

He's still smiling, but I'm worried suddenly that he's making this about us. I open my eyes and jump slightly.

Brett has pushed himself up on his elbows and rolled onto his side so he's looming right over me. He doesn't look in the least bit pissed off.

Now, I see he's just teasing me. "I don't chase guys. They're the ones who chase me." I grin.

Brett laughs softly. He reaches out and rubs his hand lightly over my stomach.

My body responds instantly to his touch, my skin puckering beneath my dress and my heartbeat speeding up.

"That sounds more likely to be the case." He gets to his knees and in one smooth movement, he's kneeling between my legs, his hands on my sides. "Ok, so pretend I was chasing you.

Now I've caught you. What happens next?" he asks, looking down at me with a lust filled grin.

I know where this is going to go, and I know we're treading on dangerous ground. Can I risk this happening again? I know I shouldn't, but we got past it last time and still managed to work together effectively. So this time, I think we'll both handle it a whole lot better. "That depends on what you want to happen," I say, pushing myself back up onto my elbows.

I expect Brett to lean down and kiss me, but he surprises me.

Instead of kissing me, he starts to tickle my ribs, making me shriek with laughter and try to squirm away. He holds me tightly, so there's nowhere I can roll to and escape his fingers. "What if they decide they want to tickle you?" He laughs.

He's still ticking me and I laugh and wriggle, managing to get onto my side, but no further. I am both desperate for the tickling to stop, and willing him to keep touching me. I see a way to make both things happen and I wait for the right moment. I roll back onto my back, still laughing and trying to ignore the tickling sensation in my ribs. I flick my legs up, wrapping them around Brett's waist and throwing myself to one side. "This happens!" I laugh as I manage to get Brett onto his back.

As he peers up at me, the laughter dies on his face and that lustful look is back in his eyes.

Suddenly, I'm very much aware that I am straddling Brett's thighs, my dress hiked up to my waist. I clear my throat and start to move to one side.

Brett is faster and before I know it, he's sitting up, his arms wrapped around my shoulders. He pulls me closer and I'm sitting in his lap. I wrap my legs around his waist, throwing caution to the wind. He leans down and his lips brush against mine.

I wrap my arms around him, shifting in his lap to find a comfortable spot. He pushes his tongue into my mouth, no longer playing. I kiss him with everything I have held back all week. The anger, the pain, and the overwhelming, all consuming desire I feel every time I look at him.

My hands roam over his back, feeling the grains of sand clinging to his shirt. I untuck his shirt and push my hands beneath it. I take several grains of sand with me, making his back feel rough and scratchy but I don't care and if it bothers him.

Brett doesn't stop kissing me to complain. His hands skim over my sides, over the ribs he was just tickling, but this time, he doesn't tickle me. Instead, he spreads fire through my body with desperate caresses. He moves his hands to my hips. His left hand stays on my hip, but his right hand keeps moving, skimming over my bunched up dress. He puts his hand on my knee then moves it higher, pushing it under my dress and over my thigh.

I gasp as he runs his nails over my skin, teasing me. My thigh is on fire and my pussy is already wet, already craving his cock. I need him to fill me up, to make me come like he did last week. I need to feel that moment of reckless abandonment, when I stopped thinking and started only feeling.

Moving my hands over his back, I bring them around to the front of his body and grasp his waistband. He doesn't stop me this time when I find the button and release it. I am reaching for his zipper when a voice yells from above us.

"What the hell do you two think you're doing? Get out of here right now!"

$$14$$

Gasping again for a different reason this time, I push myself away from Brett. I'm skidding over the sand on my ass, trying desperately to pull my dress back down.

Brett, casual as ever, stays where he is. He stretches his legs out, unashamed even as I blush a deep scarlet color. He leans back on his palms and tilts his face up to the sun. "Good evening Carl," he says casually and nods. "Stewart."

I forget my embarrassment for a moment as I frown at his familiarity with the security guards, but then I remember he owns the place.

The two young looking security guards are both blushing as deep a shade of red as I am. "O-oh. Umm... hi B-Brett," the one who yelled stutters out.

The other one looks a little bit more in control of himself. But then he wasn't the one who busted his boss with a girl and tried to kick him out. "Sorry Brett. We didn't realize it was you," he says.

"I should hope not, seeing as you tried to kick me out," Brett says good naturedly. He stands and turns to face the two young men.

They both shrink away, obviously expecting to be fired. Brett smiles at them and they exchange a glance. They don't look entirely sure of what's going on here.

I have to admit I'm stumped myself as what Brett is going to do. I mean surely he can't fire them. We did sneak in through the bushes. It's not like they could have known it was him.

"Relax guys," Brett says. "You're not in any trouble. In fact, I should probably commend you both on doing a thorough job of your patrol coming right out here."

The two security guards smile uncertainly.

"I trust you'll both be discrete about this," he adds.

They both nod furiously.

"Of course," one of them says,

I know it's a lie. It's like one of the office staff catching Mr. Connell with a woman in his office. That shit would be around the building like wild fire. Brett probably knows it too, but it's not like he's married or anything, and no one here knows I work for him, even temporarily, so I guess it doesn't really matter. They'll gossip about it until something else comes along, and then they'll move on.

"And maybe you should shorten your patrol area for the rest of the night," Brett says.

"Yes. Yes, of course," one of them says.

If he thinks anything is going to happen between us now, he's very wrong. This is the most embarrassing moment of my life, and there's no way I'm risking a repeat performance of it.

The two security guards stand staring at Brett nervously.

"So, do you think you two can get back to work then?" Bret smirks at them. "Or are you waiting for an encore?"

The two security guards both scramble away at the exact same moment, and

I can't help but laugh.

Brett sits back down beside me. "Well, that was new and awkward wasn't it?".

Before I can respond with a resounding yes, Brett starts to laugh. It's a full on belly laugh, the kind that once it gets hold of you, you just can't stop it.

It's so good to hear him laugh like this. Obviously, I've heard him laugh, but not like this. Not where he lets himself lose control so completely that tears are streaming down his face. He looks so much younger, so care free, and although I'm still mortified about being caught with my dress around my waist, I find myself joining in. His laughter is infectious and soon, we're both laughing, tears running down both of our faces.

Brett presses his hand to his side. "Stitch," he gets out between laughs.

Somehow, that just makes it funnier and our laughter goes on. When we finally get control of ourselves, my ribs are hurting.

Brett reaches out and wipes a stray tear from my face. "God Opal, what are you doing to me?" he says, shaking his head.

"What am I doing to you?" I laugh. "I'm the one who got caught with my skirt around my waist."

"Yeah, that was pretty funny." Brett smirks.

I elbow him.

He shoves me gently by bumping my arm with his. "Come on, admit it. It was funny."

"Ok, it was pretty funny," I have to admit.

"And hey, at least they weren't your staff. I can't believe I got caught by my own staff. They'll be having a field day back in the club house now," he says.

"Oh like you've never brought a woman here before," I tease him. "Even if they didn't catch you in the act, they knew what you were doing out here."

"I can hand on my heart say I have never done anything like this before Opal. That's what I mean. You just ... you have this effect on me, like when I'm near you, I just can't control myself."

"It works both ways," I confirm. "Believe it or not, I'm not usually one for rolling around in sand pits."

"It's a bunker," he corrects me.

I shake my head. "Like that matters." I stretch out on the sand and lay down, resting my head in Brett's lap. "So this effect we have on each other? You make it sound like it's a bad thing."

"Well, isn't it?" Brett says. "I'm your boss, Opal. This is so unprofessional, it's unreal."

"It's only temporary though," I remind him. "Obviously, we'll have to learn some self control short term, but once your dad comes back to work, well then ...." I trail off, leaving the rest unsaid. I don't need to spell it out to him. Once his dad is back, he won't be my boss anymore and we can do what we want. Although, maybe not in such a public place next time.

"Actually, it might be a little bit more permanent than that," he says, brushing a strand of hair back from my forehead.

I frown up at him.

"When I told you earlier I was angry at my father, that's why. Before you came to the meeting, I was meant to be having lunch with my mom. What I didn't know was it actually lunch with both of my parents where they tried to railroad me into taking over the company permanently."

"And you're considering it?" I ask, surprised to hear this after what he said about hating asset management.

He shrugs. "I don't know what to do Opal. I mean it's not what I want. It's not what I've ever wanted. And whenever they've brought this up in the past, I've had no trouble saying no. But it's different now. As they pointed out, this place runs itself, and the place in France is the same. Both clubs have excellent managers and I don't need to be involved in the day to day running of the place." He stops talking for a moment.

I don't say anything. I don't think he wants or needs my advice. He just wants to talk it through, to think out loud. I know I'm right when he goes on without waiting for any kind of answer from me.

"See here's the thing. This time, I heard myself saying I would think about it. Because how do you say no, when your father has just had a heart attack? What if I turn them down and he goes back to work, because he's made it clear there's no one else he trusts to hand the company over to. Then the stress gets to him and he has another heart attack? What if he isn't so lucky next time and it kills him? That will be on me."

I don't know what to say to this. I want to tell him it won't be his fault at all, but I know if I were in his position and that happened, I would blame myself too. And no amount of rationalizing from someone else would convince me otherwise.

He puts his hand on my arm where my arms are crossed over.

Placing my other hand over the top of his, I give it a squeeze.

"So yeah. Nothing is as clear cut as it seems. I should have told you before we started fooling around, I know, but I just got caught up in the moment," he adds.

"Even if you'd told me, it wouldn't have stopped me from kissing you back," I say.

He nods and smiles but it's a sad smile.

It makes me feel sad for him. I can't stand to see that look on his face, and I decide to try to make him laugh. It won't make this decision any easier, but it might at least cheer him up in the moment. "On the other hand, if you'd warned me you had active patrols in place that might have stopped me." I smile.

He laughs softly and the sadness is gone for the moment. "You know what Opal? I think you're lying to me." He grins.

I sit up and laugh, punching him playfully in the leg. "I'm so not!"

"Ok, you keep telling yourself that," he teases me.

I put my tongue at him.

"Real mature comeback." He chuckles.

"I'll be mature on Monday," I say. "But it's the weekend and I just want to let my hair down and have fun."

"Fair enough," Brett says then he pauses. "So how about we pick up something for dinner and go back to my place?"

"I'd like that." I smile.

Screw worrying about him being my boss. Screw worrying about getting my stupid heart broken. Just for once, I want to do the fun thing, not the sensible thing. And no amount of telling myself nothing can ever happen between us again, is stopping me from wanting him. I know I can't have him, but at least this way, I might get another *rock my world* orgasm to think about when I curse the fact that he's my boss.

15

Laughing softly, Brett gets back into the car.

My stomach growls when the delicious smell of the dinner he's picked up wafts towards me. It smells rich and tomatoey, a little spicy. I feel a little bit embarrassed about the noise my stomach is making, but my hunger supersedes my embarrassment.

"I guess you're hungry." He nods to my stomach and then trails his hot gaze slowly up along my body until he's looking into my eyes.

His gaze makes my heart flutter and my body tingles. "Ravenous," I say, looking him in the eye.

We both know it's not just the food I'm ravenous for.

Brett looks back at me, his eyes dark and intense. They flit from side to side slightly as he takes in my whole face.

I swallow hard beneath his intense gaze as my pussy floods.

He reaches across the backseat of the car and puts his hand on my thigh.

Sparks fly through my body as I moan quietly and then turn it into a cough in case the driver heard it.

Brett smirks and slowly moves his hand up my thigh, pushing it beneath my dress. I can feel myself shuffling closer to him as my skin responds to his touch. His hand is still moving upwards and I have to bite my lip to keep from calling out when his fingers graze over my damp panties. His touch is light, but the lace of my panties still rubs ever so slightly over my clit, and even that feather soft touch makes me want to grab Brett and ride him right here in the back seat of the car.

Closing my eyes, I rest my head against the seat back as Brett's expert fingers caress me through the lace. His touch is teasing, just firm enough to work me into a frenzy, but not firm enough to give me any sort of release. I bite down on my lip again as I begin to move my hips, pressing myself into his touch.

It's still not enough and I need more. I need the release that only he can give me. My own hand starts to move, responding to the command of my body rather than my brain. It slips beneath my dress, my arm brushing Brett's. I hear him suck in a breath as our arms touch. I run my nails along his arm until my hand reaches his, and then I cup his hand with my own, applying pressure, pressing down and getting the hard touch on my clit that I crave. I suck in a gasping breath, as an intense pulse goes through my clit.

Brett keeps his hand in place, but he lets me control his touch, bending to my will as I move my fingers over his, harder and faster. I can feel myself coming undone. My breath catches in my throat as pleasure courses through my body, leaving a fiery trail in its wake.

Opening my eyes, I glance at Brett. He is looking back at me, his face full of lust and I know it's not just me he is tormenting; it's himself as well. He's as desperate for me as I am for him. I see his throat work as he swallows hard.

My clit is greedy, screaming for more and I feel myself pressing down even harder on Brett's fingers, moving them rapidly from side to side. I want to move my hand back, drag my panties away from me, but I'm afraid that if I move my hand from Brett's for even a second that the spell will be broken.

That he'll remember where we are and stop touching me.

Closing my eyes again, I feel my whole body starting to tingle. My orgasm is so close now and I can't let myself go too far. I have to stay in control so I don't scream out Brett's name as I come.

I'm almost there when I feel Brett lean towards me. I smell his scent, feel the heat from him as he comes closer. He whispers in my ear, so close that I can feel his breath tickling my already tingling skin, "Come for me Opal."

It's a whisper, but that doesn't take away from the fact that it's clearly a command. I slip over the edge, losing control as my body follows Brett's order. I take in a large, gasping breath as my orgasm slams through my clit, my pussy, up into my stomach and beyond. It spreads through my full body, bringing me to life, priming me for more, and I hold onto the breath I took.

I feel every muscles in my body contract and then relax, contract and then relax. I can feel my face screwing up as the intense pleasure becomes almost more than I can bear—then it's over and I am coasting down, filled with warmth and tingling aftershocks.

It's a relief when the intense feeling has passed, but it's also a disappointment. I thought I was ready for my climax, for the release it would bring, but I was wrong. I wasn't ready for it to be over and already, I am craving Brett's touch again.

I let out my breath in a shaky sigh, and Brett choose that moment to press his fingers firmly against my tender clit. A pulse of electricity passes over me and as much as I try to stop it, I can't help it. I let out an *ahh* sound. Brett clamps his other hand over my mouth in time to stop me from screaming out loud.

"Is everything okay back there?" the driver asks as Brett takes his hand away from my face. "I thought I heard something." He catches my eye in the mirror.

I know I must look as dishevelled as I feel, but I catch myself and smile. "I'm fine. Just a cramp." I'm surprised at how normal my voice sounds. I sound a little breathless, but a bad enough cramp could do that right?

The driver holds my eye a moment longer and then he nods once and his eyes go back to the road.

Brett and I look at each other and we both laugh quietly.

"Those damned cramps can strike just about anywhere," Brett says, his eyes shining with amusement. He rubs his fingers over me again, and again,

I feel a sharp jolt of electricity go through me. This time, I manage to hold in the moan that tries to leave me. "Yes, so it would seem," I say.

I move my hand away from Brett's and he runs his fingers lightly along my panties. My panties are so wet now that they are sticking to me. I can see the lust passing across Brett's face as he feels how wet they are.

He removes his hand from beneath my dress as the car pulls onto his block. His driver stops the car outside of a fancy looking building and I peer out of the window. A doorman stands on the door to the apartments, and inside, I can see a manned desk.

Brett thanks the driver and gets out of the car with the food bag. I push my door open as Brett comes around the back of the car. He reaches the door as I start to get out. He offers me his hand and I take it, feeling myself flush. I am well aware of where that hand has just been. The magic it can make. Even my fingertips feel the magic as Brett touches them.

I get out of the car and Brett takes my hand in his, sending more sparks running through me. He leads me into the building, nodding a hello at the doorman who opens the door for us and wishes us a good evening.

Oh, we will be having a good evening all right.

He greets the man behind the desk by name and then he leads me to the elevator. He presses the button and we step inside. As soon as the doors close behind us, we look at each other and we both burst into laughter.

"A cramp? You couldn't come up with something better than that?" Brett laughs.

"I just panicked in the moment." I giggle. "Seriously, it was either telling him I had a cramp, or telling him not to mind me, I was just flooding his seats."

The laughter dies on Brett's lips and he stares at me

It's a look so intense I feel my insides shifting.

He releases my hand and wraps his spare arm around my waist, pulling me to him. He presses his lips against mine, kissing me hard and passionately.

I hear myself moan and I push my hand into his hair, mashing his lips even tighter against mine.

Pushing his tongue into my mouth, he meets mine with it. Just as abruptly as he kissed me, he pulls away and takes my hand again, as though nothing happened. The elevator doors ping open and he smiles at me, a teasing smile that tells me he knows exactly what he's doing to me.

"This is us," he says, leading me out of the elevator and down a short length of hallway.

The hallway is lined with a thick red carpet that feels like springy grass beneath my feet.

He leads me to the only door in sight and digs in his pocket.

"There are no other doors along here," I say stupidly.

He laughs softly. "That's because there are no other apartments up here."

"You have the full floor?" I ask, my surprise showing.

Finding his key, Brett starts to open the door. He turns his attention to me and shakes his head. "Sure," he says. "And thanks for sounding so surprised that I might be successful enough to have a big apartment."

"I wasn't—I-I didn't ..." I stutter.

Brett laughs again, and kisses the tip of my nose. "I know. I was just joking Opal."

When he says my name it reminds me of the last time he said it, when he told me to come for him, and a shiver of desire runs through me. I try to swallow but my mouth is suddenly dry. My pussy clenches, and my clit tingles. I'm ready for more. I am always ready for more when I'm with Brett. Even when I'm coming down from an orgasm, feeling lazy and sated, I'm still ready for more of him.

Brett gets the door open and pushes it wide, gesturing with his arm for me to enter.

I step inside.

He flicks the light on and then turns it lower, leaving a soft, romantic looking glow over the room.

The room is absolutely huge. At one end, a large kitchen area dominates the space, filled with every gadget imaginable. A high counter runs the length of it, separating it out from the rest of the room to some extent. A row of four white, tall stools are pushed close to the counter.

I can't help but picture a topless Brett sitting there eating breakfast on a sunny morning, the sun shining in and giving his hair lighter colored flecks. I clear my throat and move my attention away from the counter, away from the half naked Brett in my mind.

On the other side of the counter, a dining table and four chairs stands beneath a crystal chandelier that should look gaudy but somehow, looks just right. At the other end of the room, a seating area is set up. With a black leather couch and large matching recliners arranged around a glass topped table, facing a fireplace. Above which hangs the largest TV I've ever seen outside of a movie theatre. Adjacent to the seating area is a closed door.

I know somewhere behind that door is Brett's bedroom and my pussy clenches again. I see another flash of a shirtless Brett. This time, he stands in the doorway to his bedroom, smiling and beckoning me closer to him.

I move my eyes from the door quickly, but not before my cheeks burn at the thought of what could happen behind that door tonight. Opposite me is a wall of glass with a large balcony and a view over the whole city. Although I can't help but think of Brett pressing me up against the balcony and fucking me from behind, it still seems like the safest area to focus my attention on. "Wow," I breath the word out.

"You like it?" Brett asks kicking the door closed and moving to stand by my side.

"That view is amazing. And, well, all of it is amazing really."

Brett smiles. He reaches out to me and runs his hand up my side, leaving behind a trail of goose bumps. His fingers skim over the side of my breast and my nipple jumps to life, hardening instantly. His fingers keep moving and he runs them lightly up my neck and over my jaw, finally running them over my lips. He leans forward and rubs his lips over mine, his touch so light I could almost believe I imagined it if it wasn't for the fire he leaves behind, making my lips swell and tingle.

Pulling back, he looks into my eyes and smiles. His eyes shine as he drinks me in. "I'll go and put the dinner out," he says.

His voice is so seductive I feel a rush of warm liquid spilling out between my legs.

It's the voice he should be using to tell me what he wants to do to me, not what he wants to do with our dinner. I try to respond, but I can't speak as he holds me in place with only his eyes. I'm completely at his mercy and he knows it. I am hungry for him, not dinner. He smiles again and I realize he is just teasing me. There is no way either of us are going to try to wait until after dinner to finish what we started in the car.

"Or we could wait for dinner," he suggests.

"I could eat," I reply in a husky voice, playing along with his teasing. I lean closer to Brett and run my tongue over his ear. "But I would much rather be eaten."

16

Brett swallow hard and then he moans, a long, low moan that makes my pussy ache for him. He stalks away quickly.

Now I wonder for a horrible second if I've gone too far, if I've scared him away. Have I come across as too desperate?

I needn't have worried. He puts the food down on the counter and turns back to me. He closes the gap between us in record time and pulls me roughly into his arms. Our lips come together and I feel like we've both been unleashed once more.

This time, we don't need to restrain ourselves and our movements are a flurry of clothes flying off and within seconds, we're both naked. Brett stands back again and looks me up and down. He makes an appreciative sound in his throat and then his lips find mine again. Our hands grope over each other, both of us wanting to consume the entirety of the other person. I want to run my hands over every inch of

Brett. I want to taste every inch of him. But most of all, I want to feel him inside of me.

He's already hard. I can feel his cock pressing against me as he holds me to him. He begins to move, walking me backwards without breaking our kiss. I let him guide me, feeling completely safe in Brett's arms, knowing instinctively that he won't let me fall. Except I am falling. I'm falling for him, and I know I shouldn't let myself go there, but it feels so good that I can't help it.

I feel something pushing against my knees and my lower legs.

Brett moves his mouth from mine. "Sit," he commands.

It doesn't even occur to me to argue with him. I am completely at his command and right now, I would do anything he told me to do. I half sit, half fall and my ass lands on the arm of the leather couch. The leather is cool against my hot skin and I squirm slightly, enjoying the smooth texture against me.

Brett smiles down at me, then he gets to his knees before me and pushes my legs open. He nods approvingly at my pussy, spread wide and on display for him. He makes an appreciative sound then with no warning, his tongue is on my clit.

My body is on fire once more as I scoot my ass forward a little further and then let my upper body flop back. I lay back on the soft leather, my back arched where my ass and pussy is elevated. Brett's tongue is bringing my pussy back to life, waking up every nerve ending in me. There's no urgency this time. He works me slowly, building up the pleasure wave by delicious wave until I don't think I can take it any longer.

It's torture. Slow, agonising, delicious torture. I start to lift one of my legs, planning on wrapping it around Brett's neck, pulling him more tightly against me, but he stops me, firmly pressing my leg back down. He runs his fingers along my inner thigh as he places my leg back down and it sends another wave of ecstasy through me.

I can feel myself falling into Brett. Each wave of pleasure takes me a little closer to the place where I lose myself completely and become one with him. I am afraid to go there, but Brett isn't relenting. He isn't giving me a *get out of jail free* card this time. He's telling me, with his tongue, that we're in this now. That we're not going to be holding back.

Still, he teases me, alternating between a firm sideways movement that brings me to the edge, and then a light, lapping motion that eases me back towards the start line. My head is spinning, my insides are clenching, my nerves are screaming in sweet pain. My body craves release and I fear I will go crazy if this lasts much longer. That wouldn't be so bad though. Being driven to the depths of madness by Brett's tongue sounds quite appealing and I let myself slip closer to losing control.

Brett is back to lapping at me gently.

I moan with frustration, my hands making fists where they lay against the couch, right up behind my head. I can feel my nails making half moon shaped indents on my palms. I make a whimpering sound, begging him with my mind to bring me the release I so desperately crave, but Brett's touch is still light, his teasing still going on, and I can't do this any longer. "Oh my God, Brett please," I whimper.

He leaves his tongue in place on my clit, but it stops moving and I feel his head brush my thighs as he lifts it.

I lift my head and meet his blazing eyes. "Make me come," I whisper, my cheeks on fire.

He sinks back down and kisses my clit, a soft kiss that makes me moan once more.

"Please," I whimper.

My words seem to reach him and he sucks my clit roughly into his mouth, nipping it gently between his teeth. At the same time, he pushes his fingers into my dripping wet pussy and begins to massage my g-spot. He rubs his fingers over it, working me and then he mashes my clit between his tongue and the ridged roof of his mouth.

I have never felt anything quite like it, the intensity is too much and yet, I want more. As my orgasm hits me, I feel my body going rigid, my back being dragged from the couch, arching almost in two. I can't breathe, I can't think, and for a moment, my eyes roll back in my head and I can't see anything but blackness, the scattered red dots of my heart-beat pulsing through it.

Wave after wave of ecstasy courses through my veins and I feel like I am about to explode. My clit is singing, my pussy clenching so tightly I can feel the knuckles on Brett's fingers as I slowly come back to myself, my eyes rolling back into place.

A rush of hot liquid floods from me, drenching Brett's hand and wrist. He stands up and my pussy craves him instantly, even as his fingers are slipping out of me I want him to push them back in.

Brett looks down on me, his eyes drinking me in as he brings his fingers to his mouth and literally drinks me in once more.

I feel my stomach clench, my clit pulse. I have had the most intense orgasm of my life, but I still want more—still need more. I need Brett's cock inside of me, filling me up, making us one.

Brett smiles down at me as I shuffle back off the arm of the couch and lay flat on its length. He doesn't waste any time. He positions his body over mine and plunges his cock into me, filling me with his essence, overwhelming my senses as my body reacts to the sudden fullness between my legs.

He kisses me as he begins to thrust into me, and in that moment I know I can never let him go. I push the thoughts away, as Brett fills me up and stretches me out, making my body his, making all of me his. He pumps into me, hard and fast, making me cry out his name as my body responds to him, dragging me into another orgasm that is so intense it's almost painful.

I hear him groaning my name as he comes with me, our juices mixing together. My pussy clenches, holding his spurting cock in place inside of me and I cry out with an unintelligible, almost alien sound.

Brett gazes deep into my eyes as his orgasm starts to recede. He kisses me again and then he pushes himself off me.

I instantly miss the warmth of his body, the closeness between us.

"I'll be back in a moment," he says, his voice husky, still full of sex. He disappears through the mystery door.

I sit up and smile to myself. I guess I don't need to know what's behind that door to appreciate Brett's skills after all.

He comes back quickly, wearing a pair of shorts. He's carrying an oversized t-shirt that he holds out to me. "I thought maybe you'd want something a little more comfortable to wear while we eat dinner. Assuming you're still hungry." He smiles.

Smiling back at him, I take the t-shirt. "I'm starving," I say, as I pull the t-shirt over my head and slip my arms into it. I stand up on slightly shaky legs and follow Brett towards the kitchen. The t-shirt is like a dress on me, covering me to mid thigh, and as I walk, it slips off one shoulder. I leave it there, liking the idea of reminding Brett of what's underneath it.

He gestures for me to sit at the table.

I sit down, wincing slightly as my still tender pussy meets the hard seat of the chair. I watch Brett as he moves around the kitchen.

He puts our dinner in the oven to warm back up and he moves around collecting plates, napkins and cutlery, whistling to himself as he goes. He seems comfortable here, relaxed and at home, like the kitchen is his comfort zone.

"Do you like cooking?" I ask as he sets the cutlery and the napkins on the table.

"I wouldn't call reheating our food cooking Opal." He chuckles.

"I know. I just meant because of the fancy pants kitchen."

He heads back into the kitchen and goes to the fridge laughing. "I've never heard it called that before. But in answer to
your question, yes I do like cooking."

"We make a good pair then." I beam.

He glances at over his shoulder as he pulls a bottle of white
wine from the fridge. "You like to cook too?"

"Oh, heck no, but they say opposites attract right? Seriously
Brett, I can burn a pot of pasta."

"I guess I'll be the one doing all of the cooking then. You can
do the dishes." The grin he wears fades from his face, as it
dawns on him what he's just said.

It only serves to remind me that it can't happen between us.
There's no future for us. He turns his back, clearing his throat
loudly as I look down into my lap.

The moment of awkwardness fades away as Brett reaches up
to a high cupboard and grabs two glasses. His back is still to
me as he opens the wine and begins to pour it out. "So what
do you do for food? You must eat out a lot," he says.

"I eat more takeout than I care to admit. But I can rustle up a
mean salad?" I laugh.

Brett comes back to the table with the two glasses of wine.
He places one beside me and I thank him. He sits down in
the chair next to mine and raises his glass and I clink mine
against it.

"Here's to the humble salad." He grins.

"Hey there's nothing humble about my salads!" I giggle after I
take a drink of my wine. "Those little things are really quite
up themselves."

"You know they really are little show offs aren't they? Look at me with my healthy vegetable goodness and my bright colors," Brett teases.

I laugh again and shake my head. "Exactly. Luckily, Rita fares slightly better than me in the kitchen, so now and again, we have a decent roast or something."

"Who's Rita?" Brett asks me. The oven timer pings and he gets up and goes back to the kitchen.

"My roommate," I reply. "And my best friend. We met in college and we were instantly inseparable. Of course, we grew up and life gets in the way a bit, but we're still close."

"It must be fun to have a roommate," Brett says as he puts the food out.

"It is." I nod. "I'm never bored or lonely. But sometimes, I think it would be nice to branch out alone, to be a real adult like you and live alone."

"Being an adult is overrated." Brett shrugs. "I do like having my privacy though. I mean tonight would have gone very differently if I had a roommate waiting here for me, wouldn't it?"

"Yeah, I guess it would. We might have had to share the food," I joke.

Brett comes to the table with our plates. He sets mine down in front of me.

My stomach jumps a little as the smell of the spicy tomato sauce drifts up to my nostrils. I pick up my fork and spear a piece of pasta coated in the sauce. "Oh, it's amazing." I moan.

Brett nods his agreement. "Yeah. It's one of my favorite places for nights where I've worked late and can't be bothered to come home and cook. Night which, by the way, I will now be referring to as Opal Nights."

"Hey!" I laugh. "That's not fair. It's not like I can knock up a feast now and again, and call it a Brett night." I pause and look at him, noticing again how much younger he looks when he's relaxed like this. "You know something? I think maybe this is all a ruse. You have this big fancy kitchen just so you can tell girls you can cook, but I suspect it's all a lie. That really, you don't even know how to work half of this stuff. Yeah. I bet you can't even boil an egg," I tease him.

"Well, maybe I'll have to cook you dinner one night and show you that's so not true." He grins at me. "But you're right about me using the cooking thing to impress girls. Is it working?"

"Oh, hell yeah!" I snicker, keeping it casual, but I can't help but feel a spark of jealousy at the thought of another girl sitting here where I am, eating Brett's home cooked food and laughing at his jokes. "You must have an army of girls coming up here. Good looking, successful, and a good cook."

"You would think, wouldn't you?" He cocks his head at me.

"Oh, come on, Brett. You can't expect me to believe you don't have a past."

"Oh, I have a past. I'm not like a virgin or anything." He chuckles again. "I just don't have an army of girls as you so nicely worded it. There have been a few girls here and there, but with work and everything, I rarely have the time to just kick back and have fun." He takes a forkful of pasta and chews slowly, a thoughtful look on his face. "It's funny...After the expansion of the business, I'm finally in a place where I can take a step back and enjoy some time off work. And then this whole thing with my father happened and I'm working more hours than ever."

"Have you given any more thought to your father's proposal?" I ask.

He shakes his head. "No. And I don't intend to. At least not tonight. Tonight, I just want to forget work. In fact, I want to forget that there's a world outside of the apartment at all."

"That sounds good to me." I nod.

17

We carefully avoid the mention of anything else work related as we eat our meal. It's not as hard as I thought it might be, and it doesn't feel awkward. It feels right, normal, like maybe we're two people who aren't just connected through work.

We finish the meal and I stand to pick up the plates.

"You don't have to do that," Brett says as I start towards the kitchen.

"It was your idea," I remind him. "I do the dishes remember?"

"But I didn't cook," Brett points out.

I shrug as I come back to the table for our empty glasses and the remaining cutlery. "I don't mind doing it." I run the taps and rinse of the dishes to out into the dishwasher.

"I really should stop you from doing that, but the view is too good," Brett says from behind me.

I glance over my shoulder at him.

He's sitting at the table still, but he's turned himself towards me. His eyes linger on my bare legs.

I laugh as I get the dishes into the washer. There are only the few from our meal and I know they won't take me long to do. I hear Brett come up behind me.

Wrapping his arms around my waist, he kisses my neck. "Ok Cinderella, you've paid your dues. Now it's time for the prince to claim you as his own," he says.

I turn around in his arms, my hands still covered in soap suds. I lean up and he comes down to meet me. Fire floods me again, as we kiss. This time, while passionate, our kiss isn't rushed or desperate. It's lingering, sensual. It's the sort of kiss that can make a person fall in love.

I wrap my arms around Brett's neck, melting into the kiss. He tucks his hands beneath my ass and lifts me from the floor as though I weigh nothing. I wrap my legs around his waist and he starts moving, walking me towards the door off the living room, taking me towards his bedroom.

My stomach is whirling with butterflies as Brett reaches the door, still kissing me.

He opens it and steps through. He keeps walking, still kissing me.

I really want to look around and see where he's taking me, but his kiss feels so good and I don't want to ruin the moment, so I keep my eyes firmly closed, just relishing the feel of his lips on mine.

Bending at the waist, he lowers me, and I unwrap my legs from around him. He stands back up straight, leaving me behind on his bed.

Finally, I open my eyes and take a look around me.

His bedroom is huge. The headboard of the big king sized bed I'm now laid on is pushed against the back wall, facing the glass wall that extends right through the room. It must be amazing waking up here and being able to watch the sun rising over the whole city.

Beside the bed is a small cabinet. The rest of the room contains the standard fare – a wardrobe, a chest of drawers, a comfy looking chair. But that isn't what gets my attention. My attention goes to the treadmill in the corner, set up facing the window.

Brett sees me looking at it and he smiles. "I go to the gym for weights and stuff, but I like to do my cardio here where I can watch the world go by. It's awful running and running and only seeing a wall."

I nod, but the treadmill soon loses my interest when Brett hooks his thumbs into the waistband of his shorts and pulls them down, stepping neatly out of them. His cock is hard and ready for me. I hear myself moaning with longing when I see it. I reach out and wrap my fist around it and begin to stroke him.

He moans as I move my hand along his length.

I get to my knees, still jerking Brett off, my eyes on his. I crawl closer to the edge and our lips meet. I slip off the edge of the bed, one hand wrapped around Brett's cock, the other behind his head, pulling his face down to mine again.

I kiss him hard, thrusting my tongue into his mouth, and then I pull away, releasing his cock. I put my palms on Brett's chest and push him back onto the bed.

He raises an eyebrow at me.

I grin. "Your turn," I say, getting to my knees in front of Brett.

He groans again, a groan filled with longing.

I push his knees apart and crawl into the gap between his legs. I take the base of his cock in my fist and bend my head down to the head. I flick my tongue over the tip, listening to Brett gasp. I tease him with my tongue, licking down his length and then blowing gently on the warm saliva trail. A shiver goes through him as my tongue flicks over the head of his cock again.

Taking him into my mouth, I move my head down, taking as much of him as I can into my mouth. I suck him hard, bobbing my head up and down, and within minutes, Brett is moaning and saying my name in a voice that makes my clit throb.

I keep sucking, pushing him closer to the edge. When I know he's only seconds away from coming, I pull back. I get to my feet before him.

He watches me, his face contorted with the frustration of being left hanging.

I don't give him long to dwell on it. I put my hands on his shoulders and push him flat, putting one knee on the bed beside his hip. I straddle him, putting my other knee beside his other hip.

Grabbing my ass, he scoots backwards a little bit, bringing me with him. I grab his cock again and lower myself onto it, feeling myself opening up for him, taking him inside of me. He moans as he enters me. I start to move slowly, long, drawn out movements that set every nerve in my internal walls on fire.

He feels it too, because he groans with each slow thrust. "Opal," he gasps as I move. "Fuck, Opal."

Moving slowly, I'm bringing him to the edge of my pussy and then all the way back in again. Each stroke makes me feel more alive than the one before it as I move, knowing I am teasing Brett, driving him wild the way he drove me wild before. I am tempted to speed up, to bring myself to orgasm on him, but I hold myself back, waiting, drawing it out, taking us both to the edge through slow, delicious movements.

I keep my eyes open, looking down at Brett.

His eyes are closed, his mouth hanging slightly open as he slowly comes undone.

I start to speed up a little and he growls this time. His mouth opens further as he gasps in short breaths. His hands ball the sheet up, squeezing it into his fists beside him.

Reaching down, I run my fingernails down his chest and over his stomach as I keep the pace, not too fast yet. I don't want this to end until I have driven Brett as crazy as he drove me.

He gasps deeper as my nails bring the blood the surface of his skin, leaving pink trails across his pecs and his abs.

Speeding up my movements again, I pick up the pace, making Brett curse under his breath. His voice is low and husky, and it shakes slightly. I move faster and faster, and when I know he's almost there, I slow it right down, moving into one long stroke that brings him all the way into me and then a slow stroke back up, bringing him almost all the way out again. Then I slow right back down.

Brett's gasping get worse now, his fists tightening at his sides.

I'm not just teasing him now; I am teasing myself.

I move slowly for as long as I can bare, and then I let loose, moving up and down on Brett in short fast strokes that have us both gasping for air within seconds. I can feel my orgasm flooding me as I let myself go, and liquid floods over Brett as my pussy tightens around his cock.

He growls again, saying my name in a voice that shakes ever so slightly. He sucks in a deep breath and holds it as his face twists in ecstasy and he spurts into me, filling me with his juices.

I stay on top of him for a moment, panting, getting myself back under control a little bit. When I feel like I can move again, I roll to the side, lying beside Brett who is still on his back getting his breath back.

Brett turns towards me when he has his breathing under control. He wraps his arm around my waist and I snuggle closer to him. He kisses me softly. His hand traces little shapes on the small of my back, relaxing me. I know I should move. I should get dressed and go. We both knew this was only about tonight.

It doesn't matter how much I tell myself to do it though, my body doesn't respond to my mind's command. I feel so warm, so safe lying here in Brett's arms. I even feel – dare I say it? – loved. I know whatever is between Brett and I can never be fully realized. We only have tonight and then it has to end, but we can have all of tonight. Every single second of it.

I close my eyes and refuse to let the thoughts of tomorrow flood into my head and bring me down. I just want to enjoy the rest of tonight.

Brett seems to have the same idea, because he kisses my forehead and pulls me closer to him.

After a couple of minutes, the movement of his hand on my back starts to slow down and his arm gets heavier on my waist. A couple of minutes after that, his hand falls still altogether and he starts snoring gently. Rather than irritating me, the sound lulls me into a deep state of relaxation, and before I know it, my eyes close and I slip into sleep beside him, wrapped in his arms and his warmth.

It's almost five when I wake up and check my watch. Brett is still asleep beside me, and although it makes my heart hurt to think about leaving him, I know I have to. And I think it'll be easier for both of us if I slip out now than it will be if I wait around until he wakes up and we have to say an awkward goodbye to each other.

I lift his arm up gently and slip out from beneath it. I sit on the side of the bed for a minute and then I get to my feet.

"Going somewhere?" Brett asks from beside me.

Dammit. I thought I was being quiet enough not to wake him. I debate lying to him, saying I was just getting up to use the bathroom, but what's the point? He knows I have to leave, and I would rather just be honest than tell him I'm going to the bathroom and then have him hear the front door opening as I slip out. And I can't just go to the bathroom and then come back. I'm not strong enough to do this again.

"Home," I say, turning to face him. I am once more assaulted by how good he looks. Even now with his hair all mussed up and his face still puffy with sleep he looks so good I want to abandon my plan then just crawl back into bed with him and never leave. "Sorry, I didn't mean to wake you," I add.

"It's a good job you did though, or I would have woken up to find you gone," he says.

Nodding, I give him a half smile. "I thought it would be easier this way. You know, we could avoid the awkward good-byes and all that."

He pushes himself up onto his elbow and smiles at me. "But we don't need to do those until Sunday," he says.

"Huh?" I say stupidly.

"Well, I just thought that seeing how badly we've already fucked up, then what's the harm in fucking up again? And again. And again. We can go back to reality on Monday. I know we have to. But until then, well maybe you could stay. Spend the weekend here with me?"

I open my mouth to say no. To tell him all of the reasons that's a terrible idea. But what comes out instead is nothing. I feel my head nodding, my feet carrying me back to Brett's bed.

I know even as I'm lifting up the blanket that I should tell him no. I mean this is crazy. I can't just stay here. I have to leave. But I don't say anything.. Instead, I slip back into Brett's bed and into his waiting arms. And when I do find my voice again, I don't tell him goodbye. I tell him I would like nothing more than to spend the weekend with him.

18

The weekend has gone over too fast. I wanted it to last forever, and it seems the more I wanted it to go slow, the faster it went. It feels like I've just blinked and the whole of our time together is gone.

Yesterday, Brett and I laid around living room, me in his t-shirt, him in his shorts, and true to his word, we pretended like no one existed outside of the apartment. He cooked me dinner and we ate it out on the balcony, watching the sunset. I threw my clothes in his washer and dryer but even once they were ready, I decided I much preferred his t-shirt.

We spent the full day talking and the better I got to know him, the more I can't help but dread this weekend ending. It's not just a physical thing anymore, although I still can barely keep my hands off of him. We click on so many levels and while we're from different worlds in some ways, in other ways, we have so much in common that it's almost freaky.

I know that under any other circumstances, Brett and I could have had something really special together, and several times over the weekend, I've found myself hating Mr. Connell for his stupid, archaic rules about interoffice relationships. It's not entirely on him though. I still don't think I'd be fully on board with being one of those women who sleep with their boss, even if it wasn't against the company's rules.

I've lost count of the amount of times Brett and I have had sex over these last few days, and I have no idea of the amount of orgasms I've had. A lot. I know that much. I know I'm sore from all of the sex, aching in the most pleasant way possible. And I know if we could do this all over again, I wouldn't change a thing. I can live with the ache to get the orgasms, to get Brett inside of me. I'm just glad I carry my birth control pills in my purse, or we could be in very real trouble right about now. And even then, I don't think I would have had the willpower to say no to having sex with Brett.

Over the course of Friday night, yesterday, and this morning, I've come to realize that Brett makes me feel special. He makes me feel like I'm all he needs, as though I'm the only woman in the world who can command his attention. It's a bittersweet notion, because I know it has to end today. But I refuse to let myself think about that too much. I don't want to ruin our last day together by being all melancholy. Oh God, why does this have to end?

Rising from the couch, I move to the kitchen where Brett is buttering some bread rolls and whistling. I need to move around, to do something, I can push these thoughts away fully. I am so sick of asking myself why Brett had to be Mr. Connell's son, of why I had to work for his father. No matter how many times I think about it and curse my luck, it doesn't change the situation, so what's the point in upsetting myself?

"Is there anything I can do to help?" I ask. "I know I'm no cook, but I think I can manage a sandwich without making too much of a mess of it."

"You can grab some cheese and start slicing it if you like." Brett chuckles. "Just pretend it's for a salad and you'll be fine."

I pull a face at him, but I move to the fridge and grab a block of orange cheese. I get a knife and a board then begin slicing the cheese. I've barely gotten three slices done when Brett is behind me, so close to me that I can feel his body pressed against mine.

"It's no good," he says.

"What's wrong with it?" I demand, glancing at him over my shoulder and then looking back at the perfectly sliced cheese.

"No, there's nothing wrong with the cheese. I applaud your cheese cutting skills. But it's no good you being so close to me and so close to naked at the same time," he says.

"Oh..." It becomes an elongated *oh* as his fingers grope between my legs from behind, running through my slit and making me wet instantly. "We'll never get lunch at this rate," I say, already breathless from his touch.

"We'll eat it later and call it an afternoon snack," he says, whispering it directly into my ear while sending goose bumps chasing each other down my neck and over my body.

Brett pulls me backwards so my body is pressed tightly against his. He kisses my neck as he fingers keep working me. I gasp as his fingers press down on my throbbing clit. It's tender from all of the attention it's gotten over the last couple of days, but I want Brett badly enough that I ignore the tenderness and concentrate on how good he makes me feel.

He works my clit until I am so wet I can feel liquid soaking my thighs, and then he pushes me forward, bending me over the kitchen counter. He pushes the t-shirt up and I hear rustling as he pushes his shorts down. He runs his fingers down my sides and then he slams into me.

I gasp his name as he fills me once more.

I am aware we have come full circle, just in different apartments. The first time Brett fucked me was on the counter top in my kitchen, and now it's happening again on his. Or at least… against his. My pussy is taking over my brain, the pleasure from it spilling through my whole body.

Brett rests one hand on my hip. The other hand moves around the front of my body and slips beneath the t-shirt. He moves his hand over my stomach and up to my breasts, where he takes one of my nipples between his fingers and his thumb and rolls it, pinching it gently.

I gasp again, as the pleasure from his cock meets the pleasure from his fingertips in the center of my body. I orgasm in record time. Brett knows my body so well now. He knows exactly how to make me sing. I feel red hot pleasure coursing through me, taking me away to another world for a moment.

Brett pulls his hand away from my breast and instead of holding my nipple, he grabs my hair at the nape of my neck. He twists it, pulling it and making my scalp sting as he comes hard himself. I feel his cock twitching, his hot juices spurting inside me, and then he slips out of me.

I straighten up and he holds me against him. I sag against his chest, feeling the heat coming off his body. He kisses my neck again, still panting slightly.

"How was than for an appetizer?" he says, laughing softly.

*A*fter Brett made love to me again, we finally got around to finishing up making lunch. My sliced cheese was a roaring success and I was really quite proud of myself. We ate our sandwiches snuggled up on the couch watching a movie. After I had eaten I felt full, sated and relaxed. I soon found my eyelids growing heavy. I didn't see the end of the movie.

I wake up now, shocked to see it's almost six o'clock. I mean I know we haven't done much sleeping over the weekend, but still, I'm surprised and a little disappointed to see that we've slept away our last few hours together.

Brett is asleep beside me on the couch and I stay still, not wanting to wake him, because I know when I do, it's time for us to say goodbye. How the hell am I supposed to go back? How can I just walk away from him like he means nothing to me? How the fucking hell am I meant to see him as nothing but my boss again? I don't know the answers to those questions, but I know I have to come up with them and fast.

Finally, the insistent ache in my bladder makes me have to move and when I come back from using the bathroom, Brett is awake. He smiles at me and he looks so good I just want to go over there, straddle him, and forget about tomorrow, but I resist the urge to go to him. Instead I smile back at him. "Well, I guess I should get dressed and get going then." I'm not sure whether I want him to agree with me and make this easy, or try to convince me to stay.

He does neither. He comes up with a third option, one I hadn't considered. One that I like a lot, because it gives us a little bit more time together. "Or you could get dressed and then we could go out and have dinner together. I know this great little Italian place that I think you'll like."

Maybe this is the best idea. We can have a few more hours together and maybe going our separate ways will be easier from a restaurant than it will be for me to walk away from his apartment.

He must take my silence as uncertainty because he gets up and comes to my side. He takes my hand in his. "I know things have to go back to the way they were Opal, but I'm not ready to say goodbye to you yet."

My heart melts at his words, I am a little relieved to know I'm not the only one who is going to find it difficult to let go. I would hate to think that something so meaningful to me was really nothing but a fling, a few days of fun, to Brett. "Dinner sounds great." I smile.

Brett smiles back at me, a relieved smile. He leans forward and kisses me softly and then he turns away. "I'll call for a car. While you get dressed."

"I'm not the only one who needs to get dressed," I say, laughing softly and nodding towards Brett's bare chest.

"You mean I can't go as I am?" he jokes.

I shake my head, still laughing and then I go through to Brett's bedroom. I can hear him on the phone as I take off his shirt and replace it with my own panties and dress.

Once I'm dressed, I hunt around on Brett's dressing table and find a comb which I pull through my hair. I grab my purse and root through it. I find a tube of mascara and some lip gloss. It's all the makeup I have with me and it'll have to do.

Brett comes into the room as I finish applying the mascara. I put it away and pick up the lip gloss.

He heads to the wardrobe. He pulls on a pair of black boxer shorts, a pair of blue jeans and a pale yellow shirt.

I watch him as I apply the lip gloss.

"The car is on its way," he says. "And I called the restaurant. They have space for us."

"Great," I say. "I'm starving."

"You're always starving." Brett laughs.

"I know. It's like the gods saw a chance to have a bit of fun when they made me. I can imagine them chuckling to themselves and saying let's make her the worst cook in the world, but let's also make it so she's constantly hungry."

"Yeah, if you could mess with people like that, you totally would." Brett snickers.

"Exactly," I agree.

Brett comes to stand behind me. He ruffles his hair up, looking over me into the mirror.

I am conscious of the heat coming off his body, how he's almost touching me, but not quite.

And it's already back to the way it was before this weekend. I crave his touch and yet I don't feel confident enough to turn in the chair and pull his lips down to mine. It's like we've already begun to distance ourselves from each other. Maybe work won't be so bad. If we can resist each other here, alone, then the office should be a walk in the park. Except after a day or two of it, I know it's going to kill me.

I really do have to hope that Brett decides to turn down his father's offer. Maybe then, we stand a chance. I know in theory, I could leave my job, but I know I've worked too hard to throw it all away now. Brett has other options. I don't. Or maybe I do. I just don't know anymore.

"Are you ready?" Brett asks, meeting my eyes in the mirror when his phone beeps.

I nod and stand. He offers me his arm and I take it. Is this the last time I will get to take his arm? The last time I will get to touch him?

We go down to the waiting car and make the short trip to the restaurant. It's a smallish place, the lighting low and intimate. It's not somewhere you go with someone you want out of your life. I suddenly find myself wishing we had gone to some brightly lit, cheesy diner where most of the clientele are in large groups. Then I could have told myself we were just colleagues grabbing a bite to eat together before the working week starts.

We get seated at a table in the window and we both order the carbonara followed by gelato for Brett and cheesecake for me. I look out onto the street watching the people out there go by.

"Are you all right Opal?" Brett asks.

I pull my gaze away from the window and smile at him.

"Yes," I answer. "Sorry. I was just people watching."

Brett grins and nods towards a woman walking by. "Ok. See her? I'd say she's just inherited a fortune and she's already debating whether she's going to go on a cruise first or buy a sports car first."

I laugh and nod to a man walking his dog. "That's not even his dog. He walks the neighbour's dog for her, because he is secretly in love with her and won't tell her, and he hopes that one day, she'll invite him in for coffee after he's walked her dog. She never does, even though she wants to, because she figures if he liked her, he would have asked her out by now."

"Ok, now I want to run out there and tell him to just ask her out already," Brett chuckles.

"Oh, you can't do that!" I exclaim, pretending to be completely serious. "Fate doesn't like it when you mess with his plans like that."

"Fate is a guy?"

"Well sure. A woman wouldn't waste so much time with all of the misunderstandings." I grin at him. "She's just get in there and gets the damn job done."

Brett shakes his head and laughs.

The waiter appears with our carbonara which smells divine. We thank him and I taste some.

"Oh, wow," I breathe the words out in awe. "That's amazing."

"I know right? This place does the best carbonara in town," Brett agrees.

We eat in a comfortable silence and I can't help but keep watching Brett. Several times I catch him looking back at me and I smile sheepishly.

"Have you given anymore thought to your father's proposal?" I ask finally. I didn't want to bring up work, not now, but I really need to know. If he's made his decision, then at least, I will know our fate one way or the other.

Brett sighs and shakes his head. "I've thought about it, but I'm no closer to having an answer than I was on Friday. If he wasn't ill, it would be an easy decision. But I just can't have stressing him out on my conscience. But then the thought of being stuck in his life for the rest of mine, fills me with such dread. What do you think I should do?"

I want to tell him to turn down the offer and never look back. Then we can be together and he can follow his dreams... we can both be happy, but I know I can't do that. I can't convince him to do something, knowing it could cause Mr. Connell to have another heart attack. If that happened, then not only would I feel terrible, but Brett would surely come to resent me. "I think you should follow your heart," I say carefully.

Brett gives a soft laugh. "Way to straddle the fence," he quips.

I smile at him, but then I turn serious. "It's such a big decision Brett, and I really don't think I can be the one to help you make it. I have too much invested in the decision. Don't you have any business associates you trust who could help you with the decision?"

He raises an eyebrow at my comment about being invested, but he doesn't ask what I mean. He knows well what I'm talking about. "If it was a straight business decision, then yes. But it's more than that isn't it? It's not about the black and white of the figures. On paper, it's a great opportunity, but that doesn't take into account the fact that I've spent my whole life avoiding ending up at the company. And that knowledge ignores the fact that my father needs me now, rather than just feeling like it's my place to take over running the business. Honestly Opal, I'm at the point where I'm debating tossing a coin and basing my decision on that."

I raise an eyebrow at him.

He shakes his head at me with a grin. "I'm not seriously going to do it, but the idea is tempting."

"Yeah I imagine it is." I'm starting to wish I hadn't brought this up. All I have done is make Brett stress out and remember he has this awful thing hanging over his head.

I'm saved from trying to steer the conversation away from the decision and onto something a bit less stressful when the waiter arrives again. He brings our desserts, tops up our wine and takes our empty plates away.

he break from the conversation is exactly what we needed, and Brett starts talking about something completely different which I'm glad about.

As we finish up our desserts, Brett is telling me a funny story from his childhood, and I'm trying to listen, really I am, but suddenly, it feels like the whole room is closing in on me and like the buzz of conversation around us is too loud, like everyone is yelling. Their quiet laughter feels magnified, like everyone in the restaurant is laughing too loudly, right in my face. Before I know it, our desserts are finished and we're just finishing up our wine, and I know once that's done, that we're done and I hate the feeling. I absolutely fucking hate it.

I want to know everything there is to know about Brett, but at the same time, everything he tells me, every story he shares with me, only makes me like him more, and I'm in deep enough without listening to another story and falling for him a little bit more.

"Opal?" Brett says, pulling me out of my head.

He puts his hand over mine and the sparks fly up my arm. The room feels normal again, the moment of claustrophobia passing. No one is talking too loud, the walls aren't moving closer to me with every breath. It had been an illusion, brought on by the fear of losing Brett, and his touch reminds me that for now at least, he's still right here with me.

"What's wrong?" he asks.

I open my mouth to tell him I'm fine. That nothing is wrong. I was just a million miles away for a moment. It's the sensible thing to do. But I see the way he's looking at me, with concern in his eyes. His thumb moves gently over the back of my hand. And in that moment, I feel like I owe him the truth. That maybe he'll even understand. "I can't get past this feeling that I'm meant to be saying goodbye to you tonight. But every cell in my body is screaming at me not to do it," I say softly.

His grip tightens on my hand for a moment. "I know," he says.

Letting out a sigh, I speak again, "I know we both came into this weekend knowing that's all it could be. But the thing is Brett, this hasn't gotten you out of my system. It's made me want you more. And I just can't imagine what it's going to be like tomorrow and every day after that. I don't know how I'm supposed to pretend like I'm not affected every time you say my name, or every time I look up and catch you looking in my direction. I guess I thought I was strong enough to do this, and only now, too late, am I seeing that I'm not," the last few words come out in a rush.

I didn't mean to say quite so much, but once I started, I couldn't stop.

"I get it Opal," Brett says. The same turmoil clouding his eyes, the same pain I feel making them shine intensely. "I really do get it. If it makes you feel any better, I feel exactly the same way."

Does it make me feel any better? In some ways, it's good to know this isn't one sided. That I'm not some dumb girl who's fallen for a guy who only ever saw her as a bit of fun. But in another way, maybe it would be easier to let Brett go if he didn't feel this too. I would have to learn to be without him if he didn't want me. But he does want me and I don't want to learn to be without him. "I can't just pretend like this didn't happen Brett. I'm sorry."

"You don't have to be sorry," he says quickly. "But what do you expect me to do about it? And that's not sarcasm. I'm genuinely asking you, because if you have a solution to any of this, I'd be only too happy to give it a shot."

I do have a solution to this. One I never thought I would even consider. I don't think Brett will like it one little bit, and I'm sure he won't agree to it, but I've said this much, and I decide I might as well throw myself all in. Because if I don't suggest this, then I know I will always wonder what could have happened if I did. What could have become of us if Brett had agreed to give my plan a shot? If I don't speak up now, I know I will regret it forever. "Well, I was thinking that maybe this doesn't have to end here."

Brett opens his mouth to speak, but I lean over the table and put my fingers on his lips, silencing him. "Just hear me out, okay?"

He nods his head. He puts his fingers over mine where they still sit on his lips and he kisses my fingers softly.

Gently, I move them away and look him in the eye. "Plenty of people date guys they work with. It's really only a problem if we let it become a problem. I know your father wouldn't approve, but it's not like I tell him any details of my personal life anyway."

"Same." Brett smiles. The smile fades after a moment and he turns serious again. "What exactly are you saying here, Opal?"

"I'm saying we go to work and we remain professional. We both are professionals and we can do it. But after work, then we continue to see each other like this. Like I said, it's only a problem if we make it a problem. So we draw some ground rules up. No special favors at work, no flirting or messing around there."

Brett is trying to get a word in again, but I hurry on, cutting him off, "When you really think about it, it's not that much different to dating anyone else." I have to make him see this could work, because it really could. "We go to work, do our jobs, be civil and no more. And then after work, we let our hair down and have fun. Only it's with each other, instead of two different people."

I have played my final ace and now it's all on Brett. It comes down to whether or not he likes me enough to want to continue this, because when it comes down to it, I'm the one taking the real risks here. I'm the one Mr. Connell would fire. Well, no that's not strictly true. He would fire us both. But Brett doesn't want to work for the company and he has something else to go to. I don't.

"Can I get a word in now?" Brett asks with a grin playing across his face.

I nod wordlessly, feeling blood rushing to my face.

"Ok." He nods.

I wait for what comes next. All of the reasons why we can't do this, but he doesn't say anything else. Frustrated, I sigh. Why is he dragging this out and making it harder than it has to be? I've just laid my heart and soul out in front of him and he's not even making shutting me down painless. "Ok what?" I press him.

"Ok, let's do it." He smiles. "I tried to tell you earlier I liked the idea, but you wouldn't stop talking."

I feel like my heart is about to explode. Did he really just agree to do this? Is he as into me as I am to him? "Are you serious? I mean it's not going to be easy, and if things don't work out between us, then it could make things pretty awkward at the office."

"Opal, you've just spent five minutes trying to talk me into doing something I already wanted to do anyway. Don't tell me you're now, trying to talk me out of it." Brett laughs.

"No. God no," I say quickly. "I just wanted to make sure you've really thought this through."

"I've thought of nothing else since the moment we got caught together in the sand bunker," Brett explains. "And I'm aware things could become awkward if this doesn't work out. So here's what I think we should do." He pauses long enough to lean over the table and run his lips softly over mine. "I think we should make damned sure it does work out," he whispers.

His lips are still almost touching mine and his breath tickles against them when he whispers to me. I feel the warmth of his words spreading through my whole body and I smile at him, feeling tears prickling in the corners of my eyes. "Me too," I say.

He beams at me and he has never been more handsome than he is in this moment, and I have never been happier than I am right now.

It's funny, because even knowing this isn't the end for us, I find I am still not ready to say goodbye to Brett for the night, and it seems he feels the same way, because he flags down our waiter and orders another bottle of wine.

I lose myself in him completely as we drink the wine and talk and talk. We talk about everything. Our hopes, our dreams, our childhoods. We go from laughter to serious and back to laughter again so many times that I lose count. We're just swapping stories, getting to know each other, drinking each other in, and it's so wonderful.

While telling Brett about a time in college where I embarrassed myself in front of a full lecture hall, someone clears their throat by our table. I look up to find the waiter standing there.

"My apologies for disturbing your evening," he says, looking decidedly uncomfortable the way he is fidgeting. "But we closed half an hour ago and I really do need to bring you this." He puts our bill on the table and moves away before either of us can respond.

I look around and I realize the restaurant is empty, the lights dimmed. The chairs are all up on the other tables and everything has been cleaned down. I look at Brett and we burst into laughter.

"Shit. Talk about losing track of the time." Brett shakes his head and pulls the bill towards himself. He take out his wallet and puts down three one-hundred dollar bills.

I raise my eyebrow questioningly. The bill was just short of a hundred dollars or so.

"I eat here a lot." He chuckles. "I'd rather be remembered as the guy who left a great tip than the guy who forced the staff to stay past closing and didn't even have the decency to make it worth their while."

"Fair enough." I smile, standing as Brett does.

We leave the restaurant, both of us calling out apologies to the waiter as we leave.

"Ah, who am I to stand in the way of true love." He laughs.

I suspect the huge tip played a big part in his nonchalance to being stuck at work longer than he had to be, but I don't care. I feel like I'm walking on air. It looks like the night turned out pretty well for all of us.

Brett calls his driver and our car arrives back for us in minutes. "My place?" Brett asks me.

I shake my head reluctantly. "No. I have to go home so I can get sorted for work tomorrow."

"It was worth a try," Brett says, grinning to try to hide his disappointment. He tells the driver to take me home first.

The drive is a short one and it's over too soon.

Brett gets out of the car with me and takes my hand in his. He leans closer to me.

I pull back. "What are you doing? Your driver will see," I say.

"My driver understands discretion," he says.

I know I should protest a little but more, but I don't. I really want to kiss him and when he leans closer again, this time, I lean in to meet him. Our lips lock together.

Dang, Brett tastes of wine and gelato... I can't get enough of him. The kiss is tender, loving, and I don't want it to end. It sends tingles through my body and makes me ache for him. When the kiss ends, it takes everything I have not to invite him inside, but if we're going to make this work, I can't turn up for work rough tomorrow morning. I have to forget that Brett is the boss who will see me rough in the morning, and know exactly why I'm like that and let it go. I have to act like my boss is an entirely different person to the man I'm with now.

Brett watches me until I'm inside of the building.

Turning, I give him a wave before I head up the stairs. I can't believe how different I feel now to how I did a couple of hours ago. Instead of dreading work tomorrow, I find myself excited for it. I think it will be exhilarating being so close to Brett and not being able to touch him now that I know that once work is done, that I can. It's like we're sharing this intimate secret between us, like we're partners in crime. I think work is about to get a whole lot more interesting than it ever has been before.

20

Five Weeks Later

The last five weeks have been like a dream, a fairy tale come to life. Brett and I have been very good about sticking to our arrangement. At work, we're all business. No one suspects a thing about us, not even Jessie.

She stops by my office at least once a day to tell me how dreamy she thinks Brett is, and to question how I can work so closely with him without being in a state of constant turmoil.

I really want to tell her about us, but of course I don't. It would be round the office in seconds.

I've told Rita of course, but it's not like she's going to run into the office and start spreading it around. That's the only thing I am not totally happy about. At first, our relationship being a secret was exciting, but the novelty of that has worn off now, and I find myself wanting to talk about Brett, to tell people a funny story, or about something interesting we did together and of course, I can't.

It really is a small price to pay for the great time we have together though. As soon as work is done, Brett and I gravitate towards each other like we're magnetized. I have spent a lot of time at his place. I stay there pretty much every other night. He occasionally stays over at my apartment, but his place is so much nicer than mine, and he doesn't have a roommate, so we have much more privacy at his place.

The last few times I've been home I have found notes left by Gary, my ex-boyfriend who seems to be slowly becoming my stalker. He clearly has found a way to get into my building, as the notes he leaves are not in the mailbox. They're pushed underneath my apartment door.

They're not threatening notes, in fact they're the opposite – love letters begging me to take him back – but they still make me uncomfortable. I don't know why he won't just leave me alone. I mean surely, it's enough of a hint when someone changes their phone number not once but twice, just to stop you from calling them. Apparently, Gary doesn't think so.

Brett and I are sitting in my living room drinking a glass of wine. Rita is staying at her boyfriend's place and when Brett dropped me off after seeing a movie, I asked him if he wanted to come in for a glass of wine. We're sitting wrapped up in each other, talking and enjoying each other's company. Even after five weeks, the newness hasn't worn off and I really think I could spend every minute of the rest of my life with Brett and never grow tired of him.

I am a little tired now though. Not of Brett, but it's getting late and I'm getting sleepy. I yawn.

Brett laughs. "Am I boring you?"

"Never," I reply.

He chuckles as I stifle another yawn.

I'm debating asking him to spend the night. I know I won't get much sleep if he does, but I can live with being tired again tomorrow, and I won't be seeing Brett tomorrow night. He has a dinner planned with a client, so I will be able to get an early night and catch up on my sleep a bit then.

I open my mouth to ask him if he wants to stay over when a movement at the front door catches my eye. I frown and look over there. I roll my eyes when I see a sheet of paper on the ground just inside of the door.

Brett looks to the door and gets to his feet, looking angry. "This has gone on for long enough now Opal. It's really not normal behavior. I'm going to go and have a word with this creep."

Jumping up, I catch his wrist. "Please don't do that," I say. "It'll only make it worse."

"He's obsessed with you Opal and it has to stop," Brett argues. "This Gary guy is mentally unbalanced or something."

"He's harmless," I reassure him. "He just doesn't get the hint. Eventually, he'll move on. I'll talk to him, make him see there's no chance for us." I wrap my arms around Brett's waist. "Don't ruin tonight by going after Gary."

"Fine." Brett sighs, wrapping his arms around me and kissing the top of my head. "Besides, I kind of get where the guy is coming from. If I lost you, I wouldn't be ready to give you up without a fight either."

His words make me feel warm inside and the decision about whether or not to ask him to stay over tonight is an easy one now. Who needs sleep anyway? "Do you want to stay over tonight?" I ask. "Rita will be going to work straight from her boyfriend's place and we'll have the place to ourselves."

"I thought you'd never ask," Brett gives me a wink.

I smile up at him and disentangle myself from his arms. I take our empty glasses to the kitchen. Then I pick up Gary's note and drop it into the waste paper basket without reading it. I go back to Brett. Smiling, I take his hand and lead him to the bedroom.

It's not long before all thoughts of Gary are gone from both of our minds.

*

The car pulls up outside of my apartment building and I turn in my seat and kiss Brett. "Good night," I say. "Thank you for dinner. It was lovely."

We have been back to the little Italian place where we went the night we decided to give our relationship a chance. I suppose that night was our first date, because we can't really count getting caught rolling around together in the sand bunker at the golf course as a date. If the waiter at the restaurant remembered that on our last visit we had over stayed our welcome, he hadn't mentioned it. And we have made sure to leave at least an hour before the place was due to close.

"You're welcome. How about I come up and you can thank me another way?" Brett winks. He knows I have the apartment to myself again tonight.

Normally, I would have jumped at the chance for him to come upstairs with me, but ever since that first Sunday night when he dropped me off at home, I have stuck to Sunday night being the one night we spend apart.

It feels like that way, it's easier to draw a line between Opal and Brett, the loved up couple who can't keep their hands off each other, to Opal and Brett who work together and are completely professional the whole time.

"I'd love that, but I can't unfortunately," I say. "My boss is a real dick and Monday mornings are always the worst."

"Your boss is a dick, huh?" Brett asks, raising an eyebrow.

"Oh, he's the worst." I grin. "He won't let me make love to him on his desk or anything." I open the door and get out of the car, grinning to myself.

"Hey Opal," Brett calls.

I'm digging in my purse for my keys. I turn back.

"He sounds like a total asshole," Brett exclaims.

I laugh as I find my keys and open the door. I wave to Brett and the car pulls away from the curb. I step inside of the building and head for the stairs as the door closes behind me. I stop abruptly when I see Gary sitting on the second step from the bottom.

"What the hell are you doing here Gary?" I ask, sighing.

Gary jumps to his feet.

I take a step back when I see how angry he looks.

"I'm waiting for you obviously," he says. "I came to see you so we could talk, but you weren't home. I did the good guy thing and waited for you, and what do I see? You coming home at this hour, smelling of wine, in a car with some guy. So? What do you have to say for yourself?"

"Go home Gary," I say, refusing to take the bait and have an argument with him here.

"Go home? That's all you have to say? Dammit, Opal. You're running around town with some other guy, betraying me, and that's all you can say?"

"How the hell am I betraying you?" I snap, no longer able to bite my tongue.

"We're taking a break because you said you needed some space. I get that. But you seeing other guys was never part of the deal!" he shouts. "Who is he anyway?"

"Gary, we're not taking a break. We're over. What part of that don't you understand? This whole break thing is just something you've cooked up in your head because you choose to ignore the fact that we are over."

"No Opal, you choose to ignore the fact that we're soul mates and that we're meant to be together. What can I say to make you see that?"

I'm starting to think Brett is right about Gary. His obsession is scary to witness this way, and I'm thinking maybe I should have let Brett have a word with him the other night when he wanted to. Whatever I decide to do to fix this thing long term, right now, I am done with talking to Gary. Maybe I'll see about getting a restraining order or something. Or maybe I'll move to China – it's so big there, surely he'll never find me.

I shake my head and step around him.

As my foot goes towards the bottom stair, Gary grabs my arm just beneath the elbow. He pulls me roughly back around to face him, keeping his grip on my arm.

"Get off me!" I shout, trying to pull my arm loose.

Gary keeps his grip on me and I reach up with my other hand and try to pry his fingers loose. Still he grips me, his grip getting tighter. I can feel real fear starting to gnaw at me now.

"You're nothing but a little slut, Opal. Fucking other men while we're together," he snarls, his face pressed close to mine.

As I release a little whimpering sound, I wonder how the hell I can appease him enough to get him off me without giving him any impression that we're going to get back together.

"How could you do this to me? How could you act like a little whore like this when you know I'm the only man who could ever love you?" His voice is soft now, pleading. His words don't match his tone.

I'm starting to seriously think that the man is mentally ill. I can't keep up with his mood swings, how he can go from berating me to begging me to be with him in one sentence. "Gary, you're hurting me," I say, looking at his hand on my arm. He's gripping me so tightly I can see where his knuckles are starting to turn white.

He shakes his head, tightening his grip and making me cry out.

I try to pull my arm loose from his fist, but all that does is make my arm hurt more.

"I'm hurting you? This is nothing to how much you've hurt me, Opal," he growls. He has a dangerous glint in his eye as he glares at me. "Maybe I should punish you, let you know what I am capable of doing to you if you cheat on me again. And then maybe next time, you'll think twice before fucking some other guy." He nods to himself like he's decided that would be a good plan.

I'm so afraid, I can barely speak. What the hell is he going to do to me? I can feel tears prickling at the corners of my eyes, but I blink them away. I won't let him see how scared I am. I have a feeling he'll enjoy my fear, that he'll start to believe he's teaching me a lesson or whatever bullshit idea is going through his head. I just need to find a way to calm him down long enough, so I can get away from him and into my apartment then lock the door. "Gary—"

He shakes his head, cutting me off. "You've had your chance to apologize for your behaviour Opal and you chose not to do it. Now, it's my turn. I need to make you understand how much you're hurting me pushing me away like this. And Opal? I need you to keep in mind that I love you okay? I love you, and I'm just doing this for your own good."

I feel relief flood through me when the door opens. Surely, Gary will let go of me now someone else is here. Now, I can take my chances and run to my apartment. The relief is even more intense when I glance up and see Brett standing in the doorway. He's got my scarf in his hand. I must have left it in the car and he spotted it and came back to return it. Thank God, I forgot the scarf. Thank God Brett didn't just wait until tomorrow to return it.

For a moment, time is frozen.

Gary still holds my arm too tightly, but we're both looking at Brett now.

Brett is looking right back at us, the realization of what is happening here slowly registering on his face. He goes from casual to raging in the blink of an eye.

Time starts to move normally again, when Brett takes a step forward. The door slams shut behind him as he takes hold of Gary, grabbing his shirt in two fists. "Take your fucking hand off her right now," he says in a low and dangerous voice.

Gary starts. "But—"

"Now!" Brett shouts.

Gary releases my arm.

Instinctively, I rub the sore spot with my other hand. I can already see the bruises where his fingers dug into me.

Brett puts one arm across Gary's throat and slams him against the wall. He pins him in place and turns to me. He holds my scarf out to me with his other hand.

I take it automatically.

"Opal, go and wait for me upstairs," Brett says in a tight, controlled voice that barely conceals the rage simmering beneath the surface.

If I walk away now, he'll go too far. Gary needs to be stopped, but I don't want this to tend up with Brett getting arrested or something. I step towards Brett, ignoring Gary's fruitless struggles to free himself, and I put my hand on Brett's arm in what I hope is a calming manner. "Brett ..."

He shrugs my hand off him and the words die in my throat. "Go and wait for me upstairs," he repeats in the same tight voice. "Now." He glares at me, almost daring me to put up another argument.

I can see he is in no mood for me to persuade him out of this, and his tone has brought the tears right back to the surface. If I start crying now, I am almost certain Brett will kill Gary. I turn and run up the stairs, not looking back. There's no sound from below and I realize Brett is waiting until I am out of earshot before he deals with Gary.

Getting to my apartment, I fumble to get the door open. I step inside, leaving the door ajar for Brett. I go to the sink and splash some cold water on my face and then I go to the living room area and perch nervously on the edge of a chair. My bottom has barely made contact with the seat when I am seized by a fit of restless energy. I jump back to my feet and begin pacing the apartment like a caged animal.

I hear Brett's footsteps in the hallway before I see him. He steps into the apartment and kicks the door closed behind him, and it's as if a flood gate has been opened inside of me. The tears just start flowing from nowhere.

Brett closes the gap between us in two long strides and wraps me in his arms.

Breathing in his scent, I cry against his chest, clinging to him. My intention had been to give him a piece of my mind for the way he ordered me around downstairs, but I see now that it doesn't matter. He's nothing like Gary. He wasn't attempting to control me, he just wanted me somewhere safe, so he could deal with Gary without having to worry about where I was the whole time.

"You're shaking Opal," Brett says into my hair.

I try to tell him I'm all right, it's just spent adrenaline coming out of me, but I can't get the words out yet. Brett holds me tightly, whispering to me that I'm okay now, and eventually, I start to believe him. I feel safe wrapped in his arms, like he can keep the world away from me and I focus on that.

Sniffling a little, I pull back from Brett giving him a watery smile. "I'm sorry. I don't know where that came from."

He kisses the tip of my nose. "You don't have to apologize." He leads me to the couch and sits me down. He goes to the kitchen then comes back with a glass of water and a wet cloth. He rubs the cloth over my face, soothing my skin that is still hot from the tears. He hands me the glass of water.

I take a few sips. I feel much better now, much more in control of myself. "I can't believe that just happened. I dread to think how far it would have gone if you hadn't have showed up when you did."

"You don't need to think about that Opal. I did show up. And you'll always be safe with me."

I smile at him, a genuine smile now. "Maybe I should just move or something so Gary can't find me again, because clearly changing my phone number isn't enough."

"If that's what you want, then I'll help you find a place," Brett says. "But Gary won't be a problem anymore."

I raise my eyebrow at him.

He smiles a little, showing me his knuckles. They're skinned, bleeding. "I had a little word with Gary and he won't be bothering you again."

I gasp a little at the scrapes as I pick up the wet cloth. I gently pat it against Brett's knuckles. He winces a little as I dab away the blood. "Thank you," I say. "I can't believe I was ever with him. I mean I knew he was a little intense, but I never thought he would be dangerous."

"Men like him are very good at appearing to be normal, charming even. They don't show their true colors until things are already serious. And then it's gradual, and each little step they take to cut you off from your life feels reasonable. Then it's only when you stop and see the big picture that you realize what's going on. You shouldn't be too hard on yourself."

"Well, at least this time, I made the right choice." I look into his eyes.

He smiles at me and kisses me gently.

I feel my body coming to life beneath his kiss. I pull my head back slightly and smile up at him. "Do you want to stay here tonight?" I ask.

"What about your boss?" Brett asks with a playful grin.

"Ah, fuck him." I roll my eyes.

"I certainly hope you will." Brett laughs. He scoops me up into his arms and carries me towards the bedroom.

God, how did I get so lucky as to find someone like Brett and have him want me as much as I want him?

21

Glancing up from my computer, I smile as Jessie comes flouncing into my office.

She throws herself into the chair opposite mine, leaning back in it and putting her hands behind her head. "Morning." Jessie smiles. "How is the ever delightful Brett this morning?"

"You know when you come to someone's office, you're supposed to ask them how they are, not ask about someone else." I smile back.

"Ah, I can see how you are. You're fine," Jessie says waving a hand at me. She peers at me suddenly, leaning forward in the chair and resting her elbows on my desk.

I feel a moment of paranoia seize me. Do I have something on my face or something?

Then Jessie grins at me. "In fact, you're more than fine. You're positively glowing. You're seeing someone aren't you?"

"No," I say quickly, my cheeks heating up. "Maybe I always glow and you've just never noticed before."

"Oh, dream on, honey!" Jessie laughs. "No one glows like that unless they're getting some. Now, tell me all the details."

"There's really nothing to tell," I say firmly. "And if you don't mind, I really have to get this report finished. Mr. Connell is coming in today and I know he'll want to see it."

"Fine," Jessie says, standing as she's still grinning. "But don't think for a minute you're off the hook. I won't forget to circle back to this." She leaves my office without a protest.

I know for a fact she really won't forget about this though. Great. Now I'm going to have to invent a boyfriend and just hope Jessie doesn't start suggesting we go on double dates or anything like that.

I shake the thought away, thinking again of Brett and how much part of me wishes our relationship didn't have to remain a secret. Hopefully, it won't have to for much longer.

Mr. Connell is coming in today and Brett has confided in me that he thinks he will be pushing him for an answer as to whether or not he wants to take over the company. Brett told me he's still in two minds about it, and that the majority of the decision will lay in how well his father looks, like if he is recovering from his heart attack.

Mr. Connell has been given the green light to return to work after eight weeks, and it has been almost six now, so hopefully, Brett will be able to tell whether or not he thinks his father can handle the stress of the job again or not. I want him to be okay for obvious reasons, but now there's so much more riding on it, and I feel guilty suddenly for being so selfish.

I spend some time working on my report, trying not to get my hopes up that Brett is going to turn down the job. If he doesn't, I know I will have a big decision to make.

Brett and I can't spend our whole lives in a secret relationship, so if he stays here, then I am left with two choices. I can either end things with Brett, or leave my job. Neither of the options sound particularly appealing to me, but I know that no matter what happens, I can't bring myself to end things with Brett.

So really I don't have a big decision to make. I already know what I'll do. I just have to find a job that suits me as well as this one does. I know that won't be easy, but Brett is worth it and besides, it might not even come to that yet.

After I've finished the report, I take a late lunch break, knowing there's less chance of me bumping into Jessie that way and being grilled again. If all goes well today, I'll be able to tell her the truth soon enough. She will be so jealous.

The rest of the afternoon goes by slowly, even though I have kept myself plenty busy. The hands of the clock finally read 4.25. I go and prop my office door open so I can see when Mr. Connell comes in.

Of course, Brett's secretary can greet him and make him his coffee – it is her job after all - but I want to do it. I have worked for the man for a long time, and while it's been great having Brett here obviously, I do kind of miss Mr. Connell.

He appears at a minute to half past four, exactly on time to get to Brett's office for dead on half past, exactly as I knew he would.

Rising up, I rush out of my office to greet him, "Mr. Connell, it's fantastic to see you up and about. You look great."

And it's true. He really does. The color is back in his face and he's lost a couple of pounds. He's never looked healthier really.

I feel a spark of hope in my stomach.

"Thanks Opal. It's nice to see you too," he says. "The missus has me on a diet you know. It's so nice to get out from under her feet and be free to have something I really want."

"Coffee and a muffin?" I ask, taking the hint.

"Ah, I knew there was a reason I'd kept you around all of these years. That would be great, thanks."

Smiling to myself, I head towards the kitchen. I make Mr. Connell his coffee and I make Brett one too. I put two muffins on a plate then load a tray with the cups and the plates. I head for Brett's office. Or is it Mr. Connell's office again, now? Oh, how I hope so.

I'm humming to myself when I reach Brett's office door. I stop abruptly when I hear shouting coming from inside. I know I should knock immediately and let them know I'm here, but I can't help but pause and see what they're fighting about now. I tell myself it's okay, because Brett will tell me eventually anyway.

"Why do you have to be so damned stubborn?" Mr. Connell shouts. "After everything, can't you just take this damned job and stop being a baby about it?"

"I'm not being a baby about it. I've told you I don't want the job. I'm happy to stay on for a few weeks while you find a replacement for me if you don't want to come back yourself, but that's it."

"That's it? You're still not going to give me a reason for it?"

"It's complicated," Brett says.

I hear a noise behind me and I realize Brett's secretary is returning to her desk.

She pauses and peers at me

I smile at her, acting like I haven't just been caught listening at the door. "I'm just bringing them some refreshments," I say, nodding down to the tray in my hand.

"Brett told me he didn't want anything," she says, frowning as she takes her seat at her desk. "I'm sorry, I didn't realize it was because he had already roped you into doing it."

"Brett doesn't know, I don't think. Oh well, he can just leave his. Mr. Connell asked me for coffee and a muffin on his way in," I explain. I don't want her to think Brett doesn't trust her with something as simple as making coffee and sought me out instead of her. I turn back to the door and knock lightly on it.

"Come in," Brett and Mr. Connell both shout together.

Mr. Connell might not want to come back to work here, but he still sees this as his office. I can't help but smile. I suppose I would still think of my office as mine if I moved to a different office somewhere.

I wipe the smile off my face as I open the door and step into the room. I move to the desk and the door starts to close behind me. I can feel the tension in the room.

Both of the men have stopped talking and are watching me as I carefully place the tray on the desk.

"I'm sorry to have made you do this unnecessarily Opal, but unfortunately, I have to leave," Mr. Connell says to me.

"Oh, it's alright, it was no problem," I tell him. I start for the door, but I have barely moved an inch when Brett gets up. He takes my wrist gently in his hand to stop me from leaving. I look up at him questioningly. He smiles and wraps his arm around my waist. I feel myself blushing. I go to push him off, but I think better of it. It's not like he's telling his father about us. He's just going to say I'm a good personal assistant or something, and if I shove him off, it's going to look really odd.

"Actually father, the reason I can't stay on here? It's not that complicated," Brett says to Mr. Connell. "I can't take over the company because I am in love with Opal and I want to pursue a relationship with her. She is far more valuable to the company than I and so it makes sense that I'm the one to go."

I feel like the floor has just lurched beneath my feet. I can't believe Brett has just done this. I want the ground to open up and swallow me.

"Stop this nonsense at once!" Mr. Connell snaps. "You expect me to believe that Opal would be this unprofessional?" He stands up as he says it and stares at us for a moment. His face changes as he takes us in. Something in the way Brett and I fit together, even when I'm so mad I want to rip his head off, must make Mr. Connell see that there's some truth to Brett's words. Mr. Connell shakes his head.

He looks so disappointed in us that I feel like crying. I have never let him down before, but now I have, it's certainly been done in style.

Mr. Connell doesn't say a word to either of us. He turns and leaves the office, slamming the door behind him.

I finally find that I can move again, and I shrug Brett's arm off my waist. "Are you fucking kidding me Brett?" I shout.

He looks surprised by my anger. "I thought you would be pleased," he says. "You said you hate having to keep our relationship a secret and now, we don't have to. There's no danger of my father ever asking me to take over the company again, and we can be together properly."

"Oh right, I see," I say. "And the fact I'm going to get fired isn't important enough to worry about?"

"Don't worry about that," Brett says. "I'm having dinner with my mom tonight. I'll talk to her and she'll make sure my father doesn't fire you. Plus, I've just reminded him how valuable you are to him."

"You're missing the point Brett," I snap angrily. "I don't want to not get fired because your mom begs for me to keep my job. And I did want people to know about us. But not like this. I wanted us to tell people on our terms, when we were both ready. How would you have felt if I'd just blurted it out like that without discussing it with you first?"

"I'm sorry Opal. I didn't think of that. I just thought that this way, my dad could see why I don't want to take over the company and honestly, I didn't think you'd be so mad."

"God Brett, how can you be this fucking selfish? You used me to score points with your dad. Well, nice one. It looks like you really did shock him." I turn to head for the door. I don't know if I'm more pissed off at Brett for doing this, or more pissed off at myself for thinking he was different. I turn back, giving a bitter laugh. "You know something? If you'd decided to stay here, I was going to find another job somewhere else, so we could be together properly."

"Well, maybe this isn't so bad then, if you were thinking of leaving anyway," Brett states.

It's like he's trying to get me to explode with rage. I shake my head, my anger making me mute for a moment. I make a sound that's half a moan and half a scream, the sound of the frustration inside of me spilling out.

I thought saying that I was ready to take such a big step for him would make him realize how badly he has fucked up, but it seems like I really don't know Brett at all. I find my voice again, "That would have been my choice. How can you not see that backing me into a corner and forcing me to leave the company isn't a good thing? How can you possibly think I wanted any of this to come out like this?"

"Look, I said I'm sorry and I am. Don't worry. I'll fix this."

"I don't want you to fix it. I wanted you to not break it in the first fucking place?" I shout. "You know what? I can't even look at you right now." I start for the door again. This time, I have it half open when something occurs to me. I let go of the door handle, letting the door close again for a second. I turn back to Brett.

He looks so hurt and so confused that this has spiralled out of control so much that it takes everything in me not to go to him and wrap him in my arms, but I can't do that.

Not after what he's just done. It's not just that he has put my job in jeopardy. I did that myself when I started seeing Brett and I always knew I was risking getting fired. It's the fact he used me to wriggle out of this job, that he humiliated me in front of Mr. Connell. And the fact that he can't seem to see what was so wrong about that. "Did you mean it?" I demand.

"Mean what? That I can fix this? Yes, I …"

"No, no that," I say, cutting him off in the middle of his sentence. "You told your father you were in love with me. Did you mean that?"

"I—it was a bad choice of words. But I really do want to be with you. Please, can we work this out?" he says.

I feel my heart break as I hear his words. Hearing him say he meant it would have been the one thing that could have maybe made this okay. People do and say crazy things when they're in love, and I couldn't have stayed mad at him if he'd meant the words. But he didn't. He used them for shock value to piss his father off.

"I don't know. Maybe," I say. "But not right now. Right now when I see you, I feel this … this anger inside. I need some time alone to process all of this before I can even consider forgiving you."

"Opal, wait," Brett says.

He's still talking when I open the door and this time, I don't look back. I just leave. It's after five now, so I go back to my office to collect my coat and my purse. I can't just sit here stewing on this, and if Brett follows me to my office, then I'll have to play nice with him in case anyone over hears us. I can't do that. Not tonight.

I leave the building and head home. Rita isn't home yet and I am pleased about that. I need some time alone to really process all of this. I just can't believe Brett would do this to me. I guess it just shows how different we really are. He can afford to walk away from any job and it wouldn't matter to him. I can't, but Brett can't seem to fathom that. And apparently, he thinks that it's okay to say he loves me when he clearly doesn't.

My phone rings and I fish it out of my purse. It's Brett. I roll my eyes and cut off the call. Apparently, not only is he making career decisions for me now, but he's also decided that when I say I don't want to talk to him, that I don't really get a choice in the matter.

I slam my phone down on the chair arm, but it beeps again before it's even out of my hand, a text message this time. I ignore the insistent beeping, trying to tempt me into looking at the message.

Resting my head against the chair back, I close my eyes. I just need to put Brett out of my head and think about something else until I can look at this without anger clouding my judgement. Maybe then I can get some perspective on it.

I open my eyes a bit and peer at my phone on the chair arm. I sigh and snatch it up. I'm not going to be able to not think about Brett when I know I have a message from him that's unread. I read the message.

'Opal, I know I fucked up and I'm sorry. But please don't shut me out. We need to talk about this, to work it out.'

I sigh again. I debate calling him, but even the thought of hearing his voice brings an all consuming anger surging back to the surface. If we talk about this now, I'm going to let that fury take over, and I'll end up saying something I can't take back. Instead of calling him, I send him a text back.

'We will talk about this. But not right now. Please respect my wishes. We'll talk tomorrow after work.'

Pressing send, I wait for his reply. Nothing comes and my phone sits there silently, taunting me. Why isn't Brett texting me back? Is he really willing to throw our whole relationship away because I asked for one night to think about things and gain some perspective?

I shake my head at myself. I told him I needed to not talk about this now and he's not trying to make me talk about it. How can I vilify him for not respecting my wishes, and then vilify him for respecting them too? I can't have it both ways. He's just giving me the space I asked for.

Somehow, this knowledge calms me down a little bit. What he did was thoughtless and stupid, but surely I can get past it. I mean it's not like he cheated on me, or smacked me or anything like that. I'll just have to make him see that I won't tolerate him pulling another stunt like that ever again. And maybe it is too soon to be talking about loving each other, even if I do already feel like I love Brett.

22

I pause outside of the building as I arrive at work at my usual time. I know today is going to be hard. Like... really hard. I have just about gotten used to being around Brett at work and pretending like he is nothing more than just my boss, but that had been when I wasn't mad at him. I have mostly calmed down now though. I'm still not happy about what Brett had done yesterday, but I am over wanting to scream in frustration and punch him in the mouth. I hope that doesn't change when I see him again.

I can't complain if there is a little awkwardness between us, because while Brett's actions caused it, I'm the one who refused to speak to him about it last night. I'm trying to force myself to step into the building and act normally when a voice rings out behind me.

"Hey, Opal."

Turning around, I smile. A fake smile that I hope doesn't look fake. It's Jessie and she'll know instantly if I'm not my usual self. And she won't let it go until I tell her what's wrong and I don't think I could come up with something convincing on the spot like this.

"Are you all right?" she asks.

"Sure. Why wouldn't I be?" I reply.

"Well, you're just kind of standing here for no apparent reason. Who are you waiting for?" she asks, frowning at me.

"You," I say quickly. "I was waiting for you. I saw you behind me in the reflection in the window."

"*Okkkk*," Jessie says, drawing the word out like she's not entirely convinced I'm telling the truth.

I start walking into the building, needing to just act normally. Maybe it's a good thing Jessie appeared when she did and forced me to make a move, or I'd probably still be standing there at lunch time.

Jessie follows me into the building and falls into step beside me as we make our way over to the elevators. "I know why you were waiting for me." She grins. "You want the gossip don't you?"

"You got me." I laugh, not caring a jot who Jessie thinks is sleeping with who, but thinking it gives me a good reason for my weird loitering outside.

"Word is Mr. Connell and Brett had a big bust up yesterday," Jessie whispers, leaning in close, her eyes sparkling like they always do when she has a particularly juicy morsel to share.

"Who told you that?" I try to keep my voice neutral and casual, but it comes out a little sharp.

Jessie frowns at me. Her frown turns into a smile as she shakes her head. "Someone's jealous that Brett is keeping secrets. I know you're his personal assistant, but according to what I've heard, it was a personal fight, so it's not like he had to tell you or anything. And in his defense, he probably doesn't know half of the company is talking about it."

Personal is an understatement. God how much does she know?

"His secretary said they were yelling at each other, but she couldn't really hear what was being said. And then you showed up and the yelling stopped. Didn't you hear anything?"

I shake my head trying to look innocent. I have to give her something though, or she'll know I'm trying to cover something up. "No, but there was a bit of an atmosphere when I took their refreshments in."

"Well, Mr. Connell apparently stormed out muttering under his breath about Brett being an ungrateful little brat who can't keep his dick in his pants. It sounds like he's been caught fucking one of the secretaries or something doesn't it?" Jessie asks.

The elevator arrives and we step in. I can feel my palms sweating and I know I'm blushing. I press the button for our floor, momentarily turning my back on Jessie while trying to get myself under control. "Maybe it was just an expression," I say, facing Jessie again, hoping I look normal. "Or maybe Mr. Connell isn't happy about Brett's choice of girlfriend or something. It doesn't mean she works here."

"Oh, she so does," Jessie says. "I bet it's that cute little Asian girl, you know, the temp. Didn't Brett hire her? Maybe that's why."

"Shh," I say, although we're in the elevator on our own. "Shit like that gets people fired, Jess."

"Well yeah, if anyone hears, but I'm assuming you're not going to go up to your office and call Mr. Connell and tell him it's her."

I shake my head.

Jessie grins at me, a wide grin and her eyes full of mischief. "Maybe it's not her. Maybe it's you. What with that glow you had yesterday and all."

"Don't even go there," I say.

"I know, I know. You would never risk your career like that, and I know you wouldn't want to be that girl that everyone's talking about. You still haven't told me about your mystery man though."

"There's nothing to tell," I say, glad to be off the topic of who Brett might be sleeping with, even if that means we've moved on to who I'm sleeping with. "It was just a fling."

The doors ping open and I'm relieved that I will soon be cocooned up in my office, hidden way from the world.

"You should have more flings. They suit you," Jessie says as she heads towards her own work station.

I laugh and head for my office. God, that was awkward. And that's going to be nothing compared to facing Brett. I'm debating having words with the secretary though. She should know better than to pass on gossip like that, but I decide against it. It will definitely make it look like I have something to hide, and that's the last thing I need anyone to be thinking.

I go to my office and close the door. I take my coat off and sit down. I'm just going to keep my head down and do my work. It's only one day of awkwardness. Brett and I will talk after work and hopefully, we can put this whole mess behind us.

Opening up my email, I start responding to messages. The third email I open is from a client and there is a financial report attached to it.

"Shit," I mutter under my breath.

Brett has been waiting for this information and he told me the second it came, to print off the file and take it to him as a priority. I was really hoping to avoid him for as long as possible today. It's barely nine a.m. and I already have to face him.

I debate just forwarding the email to him. He's perfectly capable of using the printer himself, but I ask myself if I would do that to Mr. Connell and the answer is of course, a resounding no. If I do that to Brett, I will be doing exactly what we said we can't do; taking liberties because of our relationship.

Printing the file out, I go and retrieve it. I sit back down at my desk holding it for a minute. The paper is still warm from the printer. Maybe I should just deal with the other emails and try to time it, so I can leave the file on Brett's desk when he goes for a coffee or bathroom break.

I know I can't do that though. Our clients have a nasty habit of making us wait for weeks for information from them, and then calling us minutes after they've finally sent it, to find out what we're going to do with it. If Brett is blindsided by a client because I sat on a file, he'll be rightfully angry with me.

With a sigh, I stand up, knowing I just have to get this over with. I make my way to Brett's office, pleased to see that his secretary isn't here yet, because it would be hard for me to be nice to her, knowing she's spreading rumours around the firm about Brett and Mr. Connell and inadvertently, me.

I knock on the office door and take a deep breath, wiping my sweaty palms down my skirt, something I haven't had to do for weeks when approaching the office. I hear a grunt from inside and I take it to be a come in. I push the door open and step in, my head held high.

I do a double take when I see not Brett sitting behind the desk, but Mr. Connell.

"Good morning Opal," he says curtly. "What can I do for you?"

Realizing I'm just standing there staring at him like an idiot, I force myself to smile at him. "Welcome back Mr. Connell," I say.

He nods to me.

I want to ask him what's going on. Why he's back and where Brett is. I can't do any of that though. He's looking at me questioningly and I catch myself staring mutely at him again. "Brett has been waiting on this file for the Leeson account," I say, handing Mr. Connell the file. "Do you need me to catch you up on it?"

"No thank you, I'm sure I can work it out," Mr. Connell replies. "I'll be mostly spending today catching up on everything, so please don't disturb me unless it's absolutely necessary. You can leave any reports or files with my secretary and I'll get to them tomorrow."

"Ok," I open my mouth to say something I know I'll regret, but he cuts me off.

"Thank you Opal, that will be all," he says.

Nodding, I scurry out of the office. It's not until I am back in my own office, leaning against the closed door that I dare to breathe properly again. So Mr. Connell fired Brett then. Surely, I'll be next. But he didn't give any indication of it in there. In fact, he was normal with me. A little cool perhaps, but normal. If he intended to fire me, surely he would have done it already.

I decide that the only thing to do is to work through my, to do list like I normally would until I'm told otherwise. I sit down behind my desk. I pause as I go back to my emails. I pick my purse up and pull my cell phone out. Maybe there's a message from Brett explaining what's going on.

There's nothing. I know I told him I wasn't ready to talk to him, but a head's up to the fact I was coming in to his father today instead of him would have been nice. I feel myself getting angry at Brett again. I put my phone away quickly and go back to my emails before I can let my temper distract me.

The rest of the day runs pretty smoothly. I keep my head down and get on with my work. When five o'clock approaches, I start to think that maybe everything will be all right. Maybe I'll get to keep my job after all and Mr. Connell is just going to pretend like none of this ever happened.

The phone on my desk rings and I see the call is coming from Mr. Connell's office. Maybe he does need me to go over that file I took him this morning after all. I pick up the phone. "Yes Mr. Connell," I say.

"Opal, can you come in here for a moment please. There's something important we need to discuss."

"Of course," I say.

He cuts the call off.

My stomach cramps and sweat breaks out on my palms again. I let my guard down too soon. Mr. Connell sounded kind of angry on the phone. Maybe he thought he could get past this whole thing but now, he sees that he can't. It looks like I'm about to be fired after all. And the bastard held off, so he could get an extra day's work out of me.

I make my way to Mr. Connell's office. I'm anxious, but I'm also a little bit pissed off. It's kind of a dirty trick to let me think everything was okay all day and then drop this on me now. Or maybe I've gotten it all wrong. Maybe it's nothing to do with Brett and me.

Knocking on the office door, I wait then step in with my head held high when Mr. Connell calls for me to come in.

"Take a seat Opal," he says.

I sit down, trying to gauge his mood. My heart sinks. He looks, not angry as such, but disappointed, and that is so much worse. I hate feeling like I've let him down.

"I think we need to have a little chat Opal, don't you? To clear the air as such. Your disappointment this morning at seeing me here rather than Brett was palpable," he says.

I fidget around in my seat, looking anywhere but at him. This is so much worse than being yelled at. I look down into my lap.

"I'm very disappointed in you, Opal. I trusted you and you let me down. It never even crossed my mind that you and Brett would be so unprofessional, making a laughing stock of me at my own company." He pauses. "Well? Do you have anything to say for yourself?"

23

I look up then, angry suddenly. He's talking to me like I'm a child and quite frankly, I'm getting a bit sick of the men in his family treating me like I'm some sort of idiot. I'm probably going to get fired anyway, so I might as well at least say my piece. "With all due respect Mr. Connell, I've worked here for a long time and not once have you shown the slightest interest in my personal life. And I would appreciate it if that remained true."

"So would I Opal, but you have left me no choice but to get involved in it when you are cavorting around my company with my son," he says.

"Cavorting around the company? Are you kidding me? Look Mr. Connell, Brett and I had a relationship outside of work. Now if we were hanging around the water cooler flirting with each other all day, or if we were distracted from our work, then I would say you have a fair point. But that's not what happened. The figures speak for themselves. We've seen a steady 3% increase in our profits these last few weeks, so clearly, we were not distracted. No one in this office, yourself included, had any idea Brett and I were involved with each other until yesterday. No one was talking about us because no one knew about us. But today, there's talk. And you know why? Because you made a snide comment on your way out of the building yesterday."

Mr. Connell raises an eyebrow at me, but he doesn't comment on what I've said. Instead, he just shakes his head. "You know Yvonne and I gave Brett everything growing up. We made sure he went to the best college, got the best education. All, so he could one day take over the company to make it bigger and better than it's ever been. And what does he do to thank us? He throws it all away on some stupid fling!"

I feel like I want the ground to open up and swallow me. I have never heard Mr. Connell talk about his life like this before, and it would be awkward at the best of times, but to hear the way he describes me as a stupid fling, and to hear the contempt in his voice as he says it makes me squirm.

"You know, most people would kill to be in Brett's position," Mr. Connell goes on. "But it seems my son is the exception. He's nothing but an ungrateful, selfish little brat. Maybe it's partly our fault because we did give him everything he wanted as a child, but we always figured he would grow up and see what it's like in the real world. But no, not Brett. Brett had to play the rebel and throw his future away. I suppose it's probably a good thing that he's shown his true colors now, before he messed up the whole company. In case you're wondering, I've fired him."

I did wonder about this, but I don't show it.

"I hope you're pleased with yourself Opal. You have caused our family so much distress," Mr. Connell says.

Shaking my head, I'm shocked that he somehow thinks this is all my fault. I can't bite my tongue any longer. "Do you know something Mr. Connell? The distress you're talking about is your own doing, because you have these archaic rules about what's proper and what isn't. And most people would kill to be in Brett's place. Not to walk into a company they don't want, but to have built up their own company, to be living their own dream. You seem to think Brett has let you down. Have you ever considered that you're the one who let him down? You had his whole future mapped out for him with no regard to how he might be feeling about that, and then you tried to guilt him into working here, even after he made it clear to you that's not what he wanted."

I run out of steam, shocked at myself for saying so much.

Mr. Connell looks at me with a sad smile on his face. "Wow. Brett really did a number on you didn't he?" he says.

"Huh?" I manage to splutter out.

"I honestly thought you were happy enough to have a fling with the boss and take what you could get. But I see it now. It's not really your fault, Opal. You fell for Brett's charms didn't you? I've seen it all before. He shows people this sweet side of him, keeping the ruthless side locked away, and he gets people to do his bidding and then discards them when he's done with them. I'm sorry for what I said earlier. You haven't caused any of this. If anything, you're a victim in all of this."

"I—what?" I stammer, totally thrown by the new turn the conversation has taken,

"Opal, my son isn't in love with you. He's used you. He's made sure he did something that was so far over the line that I had no choice but to fire him. And you're the collateral damage."

"It's not like that," I defend.

"Oh, really? So Brett tells you he loves you all the time then? That wasn't the first time he said it when he was throwing it in my face? And he didn't try to wriggle out of what he'd said after I left?"

I open my mouth to tell Mr. Connell he's gotten this all wrong, but the words won't come. Because what he's saying is pretty much exactly what happened. Was Brett only using me to get back at his father? No, surely not. I mean the sex we had, the connection...that was real. That doesn't mean he's in love with me though. If he was, he would have told me that yesterday, but he didn't. He wriggled out of it, just like Mr. Connell said.

Mr. Connell smiles sadly at me as he sees the realization on my face. "Moving on Opal, I don't want to fire you," Mr. he says.

I look up from my lap.

The shock must show on my face, because Mr. Connell laughs softly. "You're good at your job and we work well together. I thought I was going to have to fire you, but I see now that I don't have to go down that path."

"You don't?" I say, thrown once more by the way this conversation is going.

"No," he confirms. "I think you've learned your lesson. And you just need to wise up to the way the world works, Opal. Someone like Brett is never going to end up with a glorified secretary and I think you see that now."

That did it. I'd felt so afraid I would be fired and now I'm not, but I know I can't stay working here now. Not after that comment. Mr. Connell is always going to look at me as the naïve idiot who thought she had found her Cinderella story. I stand up. "As I'm only a glorified secretary, I'm sure I won't be that hard to replace. Mr. Connell, I quit. Effective immediately." I walk away without giving him the chance to respond, and for the first time since this time yesterday, I feel pretty damned good. It felt good to stand up to Mr. Connell.

The feeling good lasts as long as it takes me to clear out my desk and head outside. I call a cab and as I'm waiting for it, the reality of my situation hits me. I am unemployed and I have pretty much ensured I won't be getting a good reference from Mr. Connell. And the worst thing? It was all for nothing. Brett doesn't love me. He's not even into me. He just used me to manipulate the situation with his father.

By the time the cab arrives, silent tears are pouring down my face.

24

I have barely gotten into my apartment when I know I have to get back out of it again. I was still half expecting Brett to call or text me. I did tell him we should talk after work today. He hasn't reached out though, and I know Mr. Connell was right. I have been played completely.

The notion hurts my heart, like a real, physical pain that I can't shake away, and I know if I sit in the apartment, I am going to drive myself nuts berating myself for falling for Brett. I go through to my bedroom and strip out of my work clothes. I'm probably not going to need those for a while. I shake the thought away before the enormity of what I've done can hit me.

I go to my wardrobe and angrily pull out a pair of leggings, a sports bra and a crop top. I put them on, jam my feet into my trainers, and pull my hair up into a ponytail. I go to the fridge and grab a bottle of water. I leave the apartment, stuffing my keys into my bra as I don't have any pockets.

Pounding the pavement, I try to work off all of my anger and my heartbreak. I soon start to feel better, but I know deep down it's only because I'm moving, and because I'm focusing my energy on my run. I can't outrun these feelings. They'll all still be there when I get home.

I run for about twenty minutes and then I turn around and start heading back towards home. I'm going to take a shower and start looking for jobs. And I'm not going to think about Brett at all.

By the time my apartment building comes into sight, I'm down to a slow jog. My body aches and I know I'll be as stiff as a board in the morning, but right now, I welcome the aching feeling. I can focus on that instead of the pain in my heart.

As I get closer to my apartment building, I see a man sitting on the steps and for a horrible moment, I think it's Gary again. But it isn't. It's Brett.

I think maybe that's worse. He won't hurt me physically, but he has the power to hurt me far more than Gary ever has. Seeing Brett sitting on the steps reminds me of that first weekend we spent together. It all started because Gary was sitting on those steps just like that and I didn't want to have to face him.

I debate turning and running down a side street now, but it's too late. Brett has already seen me and I won't give him the satisfaction of thinking he has an effect on me.

He stands as I approach him and he smiles at me.

My heart lurches at the sight of his boyish smile, but I swallow down the feelings that threaten to overwhelm me.

"Opal," Brett says as I get closer to him.

Digging my keys out of my bra, I ignore him. I open the door without looking at him. He puts his hand on my arm and I ignore the shivers his touch sends through my body. I shrug his hand away. "Go fuck yourself," I snap as I step into the building.

Brett follows me inside. He gets around in front of me and blocks my path. He grins at me. "I'd rather be fucking you," he says.

How can he be so blasé about this? Doesn't he know how badly he has hurt me? He has what he wanted now, can't he just leave me alone? "Oh, I think it's fair to say you've already done that," I snap. "Your father told me everything."

"Told you everything? What exactly did he tell you?" Brett says, looking confused.

I can't believe he's still playing his role. "It doesn't matter. It was enough that I'm done falling for your shit. You got what you wanted Brett. You don't have to work for your father. And I am left jobless and alone. So thanks for that."

I start to move around Brett.

He doesn't move to let me pass.

I sigh. "Really?" I

"Opal please, just sit down here on the stairs and talk to me. Five minutes okay?" he says.

Knowing I should refuse him, I see his eyes burning into mine, pleading with me to hear him out. I sigh again. "Fine."

I guess it won't hurt to get some answers. Not that I'm going to believe them and get sucked into Brett's games again.

He moves aside.

I sit down on the bottom stair.

Brett sits down beside me. "What happened? My father said he wasn't going to fire you."

"He didn't fire me. I quit."

"Why?"

"Because I can't stand the thought that every time he looks at me, he sees some stupid girl who let herself fall for someone who never really wanted her anyway."

"You fell for me?" Brett grins.

I want to punch him so bad. "Really? That's the bit you're choosing to focus on? Yes, Brett. You still have it. Your little act worked."

"Opal, I'm so confused here. I know I screwed up yesterday, but this feels like it's bigger than that. Catch me up a bit. What act?"

"The act where you made me believe there was a chance for us," I say.

"That was no act. I know I should have called you sooner, but I didn't want to put pressure on you when you weren't ready to talk to me. I didn't want to be a Gary. And after work, I realized I didn't want to call you. I wanted to talk to you face to face."

"Just stop Brett, alright?" I snap. "You won. Why are you still doing this?"

"What the fuck did my father say to you, Opal?"

I sigh. I might as well just tell him. Once he knows I know his game, then maybe he'll just go away and leave me alone. "He told me how you were using me to make sure you crossed a line so big that you could never come back from it. How you could never be into someone like me. And he's right isn't he? I didn't see it before, but he hit the nail right on the head. The one time you say the L word wasn't about me. You only said it to get a reaction from your father."

"I think my father probably believes some of that on some level," Brett says after a second. "It's easier for him to think I'm some kind of monster than to believe that any of his staff would actually break his rules. But Opal, think about it. If all of this had been some sort of game to get my father to cut me out of the business for good, then you're right. It worked. So why would I be here now?"

"II don't know," I say quietly.

"Then let me tell you. I'm here because I want it to work out between us Opal. Really I do. I can't imagine my life, any version of it, without you in it."

"You can't?" I ask.

Brett reaches out and touches my chin with his fingers, pushing my head up, so I'm looking at his face. "You asked me yesterday if I meant it when I said I was in love with, and I dodged the question. That wasn't because I don't love you. It was because I wanted the first time I said those words to you to be special. And I know these stairs don't really count as special, but I can't wait another moment. Opal, I love you. I am completely, utterly, one thousand percent in love with you."

I swallow hard. My heart is slamming in my chest and tears well up in my eyes. I want so badly to believe Brett. I search his eyes and I see the truth in them.

He looks back into my eyes, not looking away for a second. "I love you Opal," he says again.

"I love you too," I say in a shaky voice.

Brett smiles, a soft smile that barely moves his lips, but makes his eyes shine. He puts his hand on my cheek and moves in closer to me.

His lips meet mine and everything is right in the world again.

Fireworks explode through my body, and my heart soars. I wrap my arms around Brett and hold onto him like I never want to let him go.

When we finally break apart, I'm a little breathless.

Brett gets to his feet and offers me his hand. "Can I come up to your place?" he says.

I nod and smile.

"Yeah, but I don't think we're going to be doing a lot of talking," I say.

"Oh, I'm banking on that." Brett laughs.

We start up the stairs, my hand still in Brett's.

"So the job thing," he says. "I was thinking maybe I have a job for you. It would involve you being in my apartment a lot, and mostly being naked," he says, grinning at me.

"You realize there's a name for that job right? A whore." I shake my head as I giggle.

Brett laughs. "Yeah, that sounded way better in my head. Seriously though, I can call a few associates for you and see if there's anything out there that would suit you."

"Tomorrow," I say. "For now, let's just forget everything except the two of us."

We reach my apartment door.

I open it and we go inside.

Brett pulls me into his arms, the second the door closes behind us. "I'm going to spend every minute of every day for the rest of our lives, trying to make you forget about everything except the two of us," he says.

"You know, I still can't believe we're here." I smile at Brett over the table.

"I know. It took weeks to get a reservation." Brett smiles back, purposely misunderstanding my statement.

I laugh softly. We have waited about six weeks to get this table, but that's not what I meant and Brett knows it. I can't believe we moved to Nice. The morning after Brett told me he loved me, he mentioned the idea and I wrote it off as crazy, but it kept playing in my mind. So eventually, I asked him for more details.

Within two weeks, we were out here in a beautiful villa living the dream.

Brett spends his days at the golf club he owns here, overseeing everything, and he's starting to talk about expanding again. And I am running an asset management firm. Me. Running the whole firm.

Brett wasn't kidding when he told me he would ask around and see if he could find an opportunity for me. He called Mr. Simmons, an old family friend of his, who had mentioned that the investment market in France was booming, and arranged for us to have a chat. After a couple of long and intense strategy meetings, it was all arranged. He would be expanding his business to Nice and I would be running the French branch for him.

Mr. Connell even came around and gave me a glowing reference and a personal recommendation. Since the Connells have seen that Brett and I are serious about each other, a lot of the iciness has melted between us all, but I have to admit I'm glad we're living in France and rarely get to see them. I still don't think I'm quite over the *glorified secretary* comment.

"You like it here then?" Brett calls to me, pulling me out of my head and nodding to the restaurant.

"It's beautiful," I reply.

The restaurant is perfect. It has a lovely, laid back atmosphere, low lighting and lots of candles. The food is delicious too. But really, it's not just the restaurant I'm talking about. The last seven months have been beautiful. Working in a job I love and coming home every day to Brett. Life just couldn't get any better than this.

"And you enjoyed the food?" Brett asks.

I rub my hand across my stomach and grin. "Yes, it was amazing. I'm so full now though."

"But you have room for a glass of champagne, right?" he queries.

"Champagne huh? Have you found the location for the next golf course?" I say, sitting forward a little.

Brett shakes his head.

"So what are we celebrating then?" I press him.

He smiles, his mouth curling up at the corners. He reaches behind him, going into his jacket pocket. He looks nervous suddenly. "Hopefully this..." He pulls something out of the pocket.

I wait, itching to know what's going on.

Taking my hand across the table in one of his, with the other still clutching whatever he pulled from his pocket. He squeezes my hand and then he stands. Brett gets down on one knee in front of me.

I gasp, my hands going to my mouth.

He opens a small box and a gorgeous sparkling engagement ring shines from it. "Opal, I love you more every single day, and I want to spend forever with you. Will you marry me?"

"Yes, oh my God, yes," I say, tears fill my eyes.

Brett pushes the ring onto my finger then he gets up and hugs me tightly. He kisses me.

I hold onto him, making our kiss longer, deeper, letting myself forget where we are for a minute.

Brett finally pulls back from me and retakes his seat. He smiles at me, looking into my eyes. "I'm the luckiest man on earth. I can't believe I get to spend forever with you."

I reach for his hand and place mine over it. "You've made so happy every day since we met Brett, but I think today has definitely topped them all."

"And it's only going to get better." He grins. He looks around and spots our waiter. He waves him over and asks for a bottle of their best champagne.

"Of course sir," the waiter agrees in heavily accented English.

"Do you think we could get that to go?" I ask, winking at Brett.

The waiter nods and smiles as he leaves the table,

My eyes are back on Brett, hungrily drinking him in. "I always think of champagne as more of a bedroom drink, don't you?" I grin.

"I as sure as hell do now!" Brett laughs.

We get the champagne and settle our bill. Then we leave the restaurant hand in hand and set off towards our villa. It's only a short walk, but it takes us over an hour to get there because we can't keep our lips off each other, our hands off each other.

Brett once promised me he would spend every day of the rest of our lives trying to make me forget that there's a world outside of us.

And today, he has more than achieved it.

I'm so happy I feel like I will burst and I know that our lives are only going to get better as we are committed to spending the rest of them together.

The End

www.ingramcontent.com/pod-product-compliance
Lightning Source LLC
Chambersburg PA
CBHW030907060726
47591CB00005B/1452